Evil Ricky

Old Wombs of War, Volume 2

LaneyC

Published by Margaret Chase, 2023.

EVIL RICKY

First edition. November 15, 2023.

ISBN: 979-8223913160

Written by LaneyC.

Table of Contents

To my Aunt Barbra for your support and listening skills.

OLD WOMBS OF WAR
EVIL RICKY

By Laneyc

Dedication

Thank you
Aunt Irma Bryant for your constant support

Acknowledgment

I like to thank my Aunt Barbra Morris for her love and patience.

Table of Contents

Friends

Some friends you cultivate
Others you just anticipate
Some you meet a little too late
With others, maybe you should hesitate
But with you Dear Friend
I knew
All I had to do was wait

Bobby Gearheart

Prelude

1990's – Shane

I slid into the chair at the Internet café. Dropping my book bag by my feet, I logged into the computer and began my research. I got about two hours before I need to catch the bus for the return trip home, I thought, so I set the timer on my watch. Keeping secrets from my grandparents is something I hate to do, but they monitor my computer at home. The pair love me and have raised me all my life. They, however, are old and just don't always understand me. They think it's best that I don't know where my mother is. Grandma breaks into tears every time I mention Noreen, mother's name. The pain in granddad's face is just as heartfelt. I've decided it's better to learn about her from the internet and not them. They are great people, and to bring them pain would hurt me as well.

Bing! The computer finished its search and I've finally made some progress. I found her! It took everything in me not to jump for joy like I just beat the latest video game. Noreen-Marie-Hill is alive and living in a shelter, a few hours away from here. Now what do I do? I jotted down all the information with my stylus on my tablet and stuffed it into my backpack. Ways to contact her started floating through my head. Maybe emailing the shelter may be a way in. Since the Post Office is on the verge of collapse it can't be trusted, email is the most efficient way to contact people. My heart was racing. I was both nervous and excited. I have to get my emotions under control before I return home or my grandmother would see right through me. It's no way I can lie to that woman's face, she has always been able to read my face.

I glanced at my wristwatch and could see I still had about thirty minutes to kill, so I did a little research on a side project. My Grandparents wouldn't let me have a Temple Link device, they insisted on this retro watch. I didn't mind; it was cool, none of the

9

other kids have one. With some ideas on a new kind of fingerprint spray the police department can use, I did some research. Teaching myself chemistry combinations has been a side hobby. My high school doesn't go that far, so I am using the internet and library books.

That night while eating dinner with my grandparents, I got them to talk about what it was like to bring me home from the hospital.

"You were the most beautiful baby I've ever seen, Grandma gushed. All the nurses said so. Just like your mother when we adopted her. We brought her home as a newborn as well."

Grandma wore that faraway look she often got.

"Noreen was so young and only a child herself when she had you. She asked us to look after you for a while. I was so happy to hold you in my arms and knew I would always look after you."

Granddad's face filled with anger and pain. He said, "She did the best she could for you when she got up and left the hospital. Son, we wanted to care for you when she couldn't. I only wish she had told us who your father was, for your sake. However, haven't regretted a moment with you." He offered me a weak smile.

I could tell the pain from in his face, losing his daughter still hurt. Since she wasn't dead, just refused contact with them, was worse. My decision was made, I would email the shelter, meet her, then maybe reunite them.

Months later*

The older woman rushed into the café, looking disheveled. Her hair was braided, in twin dark plaits on each side of her head, with the loose hair sticking up everywhere. She wore no make-up and her drawn, wrinkled faced reflected an age way past her birth years. The documents I pulled up said she was in her early thirties. She, however, looked to be more in her fifties. Her worn face, thin lips, a sharp nose and eyes so like mine. Noreen wore tattered jeans, shoes that look as though someone had pulled them out of a dumpster, and a tank top three sizes too small. I couldn't move or come up with anything to say, when I saw her. This reunion was not supposed to go this way.

Waving frantically at me first, she hustled over to my table. This is not at all what I expected, I thought. A faint smell of sour milk came wafting off of her as she smiled at me with yellow stained teeth. She flopped into a chair adjacent to me and simply stared for a moment, before speaking. Nothing was coming out of my mouth, either.

"So you are my boy?" She partly slurred, while giving me a toothy smile. It reminded me of a snake on the hunt for a fat mouse.

I just nodded, because my brain couldn't connect with my tongue. I was expecting a more warm welcome, like my grandparents would have offered.

"Mom and Dad did a good job raising you, I see. They may as well, since they wouldn't let me take the N contraceptive drug, to keep me from getting pregnant in the first place," she said bitterly. \"So, where do you live? I would like to see them again."

All I could think of was, "Ok," I replied. I wrote the address and passed the paper over to her.

She smiled again. "I will drop by tonight." With that, she jumped up from her seat, turned on her heel and left out the door.

Chapter 1
Year 2025: The Captured And Recorded Memories Of Rachel Monroe/Matthews

Secrets Uncovered

As we rolled along, my head rested against the window. Feelings of apprehension rolled over me as I became fixated on the white puffy clouds floating on the blue skyline. My eyes drifted out at the fields, structures, and trees representing my life go by. *Why did I feel this way? We're just returning to our current residence here in North Carolina.* We've lived in this town for the past two years, after several of our ads were answered. Our business has flourished in this town, and until today I was quite content. The uneasy feeling persisted, as though a foretelling, that my own life would have to change again. My mind drifted to all the decisions I made that brought us here in the past few years. At what point could I have changed things? I think back to where would I say the first changes in the wind of my life occurred.

It was summer, 2025. My husband and I finally have made our one-time hobby into a thriving business. The two of us are closer than I have ever let us be. Shane has become more loving and thoughtful than before, and I have tried to contain my suspicions. He has always wanted more of my affection. Even with giving as much as I am capable of, he wants more. I have a surprise for him tonight. I am wearing a sexy black lingerie number that accents my curves and gives the hint that I have breasts. Not only that, I made stuffed shells and my special red sauce Shane loves so much. I set the table with a basket of garlic bread, butter, and his favorite wine. I asked my AI (Brenda) to play my special music selection. That baritone voice of Luther Van Ross came belting out of the speakers inserted in the ceilings. I was ready for our special evening.

"Brenda, where is Shane now?" A moment later, the door opened, and I said, "Never mind, Brenda."

Shane stepped into the room and began looking around. His gaze flicked between the table, the speakers, and me. A look of worry took over his face for a moment, then it was gone. He dropped everything he was carrying and practically ran to me. Shane was 6' 3 with a slightly muscular build. He was of mixed race, a combination of Puerto Rican, African American, and Korean. The odd combination of races gave him dark brown skin with high cheekbones and very curly black hair. He is a beautiful man.

His powerful arms took a hold of my 5'9 medium build frame and began swaying to the music with me. He is the pretty one with his unique features. I am a dark-skinned African American woman with enormous eyes, full lips, small breasts, and slender hips. I am attractive, but not what people call beautiful. His kisses began at my shoulder, then up my neck, across my cheek, then to my lips. He tasted of coffee but smelled of my Shane. I could feel the enlargement of his pants that it won't take any work to get him in bed as his erection pressed against my belly.

I pulled away from his embrace and said, "Let's eat," with a flourish, I waved my hand over the meal I prepared.

He looked disappointed that the food was first. In a husky voice, he said, "I don't know what this is about, but I like it. I want to have you first." He pulled me in, with my backside to his front. I giggled as he kissed my neck while rubbing his manhood against my rear end. He yanked me around to the chaise lounge and pushed me on all fours while I heard his zipper coming down. Giving no protest, I giggled.

He pulled down my thongs, kissed my back, and said, "I love that fresh scent you have on." With no more delay, he pushed into me. He grunted, saying, "I love when you surprise me like this. Do it more!"

In a similar husky voice, I said, "I have a method for my madness. I want something from you."

"What, anything?" he panted, still moving inside me.

To face him, I spun around. "I want a baby now. I've already ordered and taken the N reversal contraception."

"Yes, yes, he grunted out, then hitting his orgasm, he yelled out his pleasure."

Once he was done, he pulled out of me to sit beside me. We were still breathless, lying back on our second hand sofa. I looked straight ahead and spoke in as much conversational tone as possible.

We were both feeling wonderful, as we were still trying to catch our breath as I spoke. "A strange thing happened today. This morning, I video conferenced the doctor at our Fertilization Clinic. A couple of weeks ago, I asked him to check on the viability of my eggs I stored five years ago, just in case we couldn't get pregnant naturally. Well, today, he got back to me with the strangest answer."

All the color drained from Shane's face, which was hard to do, all things considered. He sat totally still, with his muscles rigid for a couple of minutes. Eventually, Shane barely turned to look at me with a guilty look on his face.

Placing his icy hands in mine and squeezing, I asked, "Why did you sign my eggs back over to The Fertilization Clinic? Why didn't we discuss this? This is so unlike you, so the explanation will be good, I'm sure." I sat there and eyed him intently.

His Adam's Apple bobbed as he swallowed and mumbled, "They blackmailed me last year, and I was afraid of losing you." He stood up and paced back and forth, taking several deep breaths and releasing them before speaking. I was sitting on a park bench near the college, reading my tablet, minding my business, when a young woman sat beside me. She looked strange. I mean, I know there is a trend with these young adults to inject themselves with animal DNA and then surgically add parts. Well, she had whiskers attached to her nose and her eyes were yellow. I couldn't help but stare when she sat down practically right in my lap and was staring at me like I was catnip. I don't know what she said or did, but I woke up in a bed in a hotel room naked. She was lying face up beside me and there was a strange smoke in the room. My first instinct was to run, so I got up and began looking for my clothes. They lay close to the device, making the smoke, so I picked them up. As I held them, I turned back to look at her, and an urgent need overtook me. My desires overwhelmed me, and I really wanted to have sex with her. It was like it rewired my brain and I wanted her more than anyone ever. Shane stood and was visibly shaking all over.

I wondered if I should stop him from talking before he had a nervous breakdown. However, he seemed to want to continue the story, so I remained in place. "Believe me, I tried to tell myself it was wrong, but I couldn't stop myself. There was no resisting my desire, and I went back to her. Taking her was all I wanted, although she wasn't always willing. Her screaming for me to stop didn't deter me. I don't know why, but I couldn't make myself stop. I was obsessed. Finally, I couldn't get it up anymore. Looking down at myself, the shame hit me, and I got dressed and out of there." His voice broke as he cried with his next words, "Wanted to tell you, but my self-disgust and my pride wouldn't let me." Tears rolled down his cheeks, and he sobbed out, "I knew I would go nowhere near that park again and hoped it would all go away."

In an effort to comfort him, I began stroking his cheeks. It occurred to me there was more to this. I could smell a con a mile away, But I let him go on with his story. He needed it.

Trying to man up, he sobbed out, "A week later, a courier walked up to me when I was leaving the house with an envelope containing a recording. The voice on the device said I must come to Building 248, The Office of Animax downtown, at 2 pm concerning my adventures with a certain young lady. They, surprisingly, didn't ask for money when I got there. I identified myself to the secretary. She said to fill out and sign the paperwork. I did so and signed away the reproductive material. They gave me the video, and I got out of there and didn't look back." He cried again, and more fat tears fell on his cheeks. His voice was barely audible when Shane said, "I don't know why I behaved like that. I'm so sorry."

I know this man that I have been married to for the past ten years. He is not a cheater, but he is a man, and his instincts can overwhelm him. I stood up. He looked terrified. I punched him in the arm, then hugged him. "You idiot," I said. "Professionals conned and drugged you. Give me the video."

Through his tears, he pled, "Do you forgive my weakness?"

"Of course, but I will sort this out. I want my property back and have my revenge." I continued to hold him and kissed him.

Shane rubbed his hand through his hair as he stared at me with his red-rimmed eyes. He murmured, "I don't deserve you. I want a baby and a family."

I held him a little longer before releasing him, looking into those eyes I know so well. "Let's go take a shower." We undressed and showered in silence. After that, I grabbed his hand and led him to the bedroom.

He handed me the storage drive with an absolute look of remorse in his eyes. We sat down to eat dinner later and didn't discuss it any longer. We talked about the business we built together before going to bed.

Shane and I held each other in bed until I heard him drift off to sleep. I lay there a little longer and contemplated our life together. The business was his idea to help some elderly and bring them up to current technology. When they introduced the Drug Xenderaph

(X) into the country, it was a game changer. The drug's benefit included restoring declining cognitive functions for 3 to 5 more years. The seniors benefiting were now eager for people like me to educate them on the current technology they missed out on learning. We used various tools that Shane and me developed to help them use the old computers first, like the old touch screen model computers or cell phones, then more modern technology. Teaching seniors how to become paperless, order food, clothing and pay bills online without using the age-assisted caller sites became a profitable business. We spent a great deal of time with our individual clients, sometimes up to a year. Finally, I fell into a restless sleep.

The next morning at breakfast, Shane was more forthcoming. Shane forked his eggs and took a sip of coffee. Setting down the cup, he spoke without seeing me. Speaking from his memories, he said, "I always went to the coffee shop near the college after I left Mrs. Taylor's house because they make the best dark roast. I sat to enjoy my cup in between clients. The Cat girl that tricked me said she was a college student. When she approached me, I thought she wanted something like money or a ride. I was prepared to turn her down, but her enhancements made me hesitate long enough for her to do whatever she did to me. I felt so stupid for letting this happen." His shame in himself was far more than anything I could say to him. He was obviously barely containing his emotions. Resting my hand on his, I looked into his brown eyes. His focus turned to me and he stopped trying to explain himself. There was no further discussion on the matter that day, and we both went off to our clients.

That evening, we ate dinner and listened to soft music. My mind was still in a jumble. My barely controlled hurt and anger were tucked away behind a smile. It was necessary because I have invested ten years of my life and significant business ties in this man. I wasn't ready to leave or punish him for something that sounded like a con job. After the dinner, I was still feeling hurt but determined and cleaned up the kitchen and let it go.

We both rested on the sofa, the one we picked out together, drinking wine. "I was really serious about the baby," I said while sipping my wine and looking straight ahead. Shane grabbed my hand and looked into my eyes. "Me too. We are ready. I want this," he said, with tears brimming in his eyes. He leaned in for a kiss, beginning at my chin, then to my cheeks, my nose, and finally, my lips.

Pulling away breathlessly, I asked the AI to monitor my body temperature. When my body temperature is hot enough, it will alert me. "This is when I am actually ovulating". Shane frowned while I continued, "The hard part will be us trying to be sure we are close enough and can find a place for a quickie." I watched his lips curl at the thought of spontaneous sex.

He asked, "Well, can you put that outfit on again, and we can do some more practicing now, even if you aren't hot because I am?"

I laughed. "Of course," he would find a bonus in the increased sex for himself. Knowing this man with all his faults, I have faith in him. After that, the day continued as normal, and we went off to our different clients and our normal routine. We have built a business on educating elderly clients on the technology they need to function more effectively today. Most have recently lived independently after being liberated from long-term care facilities. They now use this vape device to deliver the drug Xenderen. With their newfound mental and physical wellness, they want to rejoin the world. Shane and I have various proprietary tools at our disposal to teach them to first use basic computers, then on to use AI devices, then various other pieces of hardware.

I arrive at my first client of the day, Mr. Mann. His cluttered home contained several stacked piles of old newspapers and books, leaving only a narrow walkway. I knocked on the door as I usually do, and he failed to answer as usual. The elderly man is typically buried deep in the house and never hears me. I entered the door code to unlock the door, then shimmied past the stacks. I followed the hall down past the kitchen, then the living room, and found the basement door. I walked down the narrow wooden steps that creek loudly with each step, and I was thankful the single bulb hanging with accompanying dangling string was dully lit. There I find Mr. Mann sitting in his Easy Chair with his arms on the worn rests of the tattered old chair. His eyes swung from the old-fashioned flat-screen TV that was mounted on the wall about ten feet away from him to me. He grinned widely, raising the deep lines in his grisly face. Even the age spots on his bald head moved with his grin. A dark-brown-skinned man of about 80 is becoming a rare sight now. The black population is on a swift decline.

Other than when I look in the mirror, I rarely see another black face today. I returned his smile as well. "Good Morning, Mr. Mann. How are you today?" I greeted.

The elderly man folded his legs down from the extended position of the chair and started the long process of standing. He croaked out, "I'm well, dear, just these old bones."

I patiently waited since I'd learned he didn't want help until he reached a standing position. When in position, I asked, "So, where is the laptop I gave you last week? I know I put it around here somewhere."

He murmured something unintelligible while spinning slowly in a circle, riffling through the clutter of boxes in his basement. I reached into my bag and pulled out my blue spray bottle. I shook the liquid around, sprayed the air, and watched as the floating dust devils glowed bright orange and danced around. My eyes scanned for things that were lit up, the orange that was recently touched. This was my formula that I only shared with Shane. We used it often. Our business of dealing with the elderly requires minor fixes like this. I spotted the box next to the door on top of a precariously tall stack of newspapers. I grabbed the stool, and, presto, I solved the problem.

"Mr. Mann, you know those papers are a fire hazard. I will ask you again, can you have them air sealed and placed in a secure location?" Shaking his head vigorously, he sat back down.

Since that was my answer, we went on with his lesson for the day. Wrapping up the lesson an hour later, I was back on the road. With about two hours before my next client, so I stopped at a convenience store to get some hot chocolate. Finding a spot to sit, I opened the drive I got from Shane. I just wanted to see this woman. Not only that, I understand how Shane got conned. Was she worth it? I mean, I didn't choose him for a husband because of the chance of competition. I do the thinking for the both of us, and I don't like someone trying to weasel in and take what's mine. Taking a slow sip of my black hot chocolate and said, "Brenda, play vid." I watched as Shane lay on top of the covers of what looked like a queen-sized bed. His eyes were open but looked strange, and he was just sitting up, but I could tell he was not quite aware of his surroundings. He finally looked around, his eyes widened and his mouth opened. Now he looked aware. He looked like he screamed when a woman spoke. She was naked beside him, puffing on a vape. I guess she had been for some time but was out of camera range because there was a haze in the room. The young woman had cat ears on her head, whiskers, and a black nose. Not a costume. It was so freaky looking.

I heard of the twenty-something-year-old trend. Surgically enhancing themselves to look like animals was the in thing. It was too weird to see it. Some, like these young women, even had animal DNA inserted into specific body parts to achieve some features. She turned over on her belly, l then I saw the tail rise as she purred out in a slow sensuous way, "How are you feeling, love?" I almost punched the window out of the car with anger. That is my husband. I finally got him almost how I wanted him, and she talked to him intimately.

She reached out to stroke him and was touching my parts of him. This was too much. He initially resisted her touch by pulling away, and a look of horror crossed his face. A moment later, something changed, and his eyes glazed over again. He grabbed her animalistically and began pumping himself into her. She was screaming for him to stop, and his face was now blurred on the camera. I had enough. I don't know what I will do, but I can't watch that anymore, yet I can't stop. Knowing the details is how to beat a con. I got out of the car and started a fast walk. I got a couple of miles away from my car. My temper subsided, and I took a slow jog back to burn off the rest of my temper. This was one of the coping tools I learned when I was in foster care.

When I got back, I drank some water and used some wet wipes on my skin. I took some cleansing breaths, started the car, and drove to my next client, Mrs. Jane Miller. I stood at the door and waited an eternity after knocking for her to answer.

The "4'11" round, wrinkled white woman came to my rescue. "Oh, Rachel Lynn, how are you, dear? Won't you come in?" She said in her pleasantly aged raspy voice of a one-time smoker.

Politely I answered, "I'm good, Mrs. Miller, remember I'm called Jack." She laughed, I mean, laughed like I said it as a gaffe. I did not mean it to be a joke, but I laughed along. "Honey, I know those foster kids called you that, but I was a schoolteacher. We don't call children by those street names. Now I've got the new AI and the other screen thing that came in. I want you to teach me how to order my groceries each week, then I will help my friends."

What can I add to that? So, I just went along, as I always do. "Yes, Mam, we can do that," I answered. I did my best with Mrs. Miller, even while I was distracted and tried to concentrate. My mind kept drifting to that "Cat bitch" with my Shane. By the time I was done with Mrs. Miller, my temper was up again, and I needed to run. My unease also compelled me to see more of the video and answer some of my questions. Finally, done working with my client today. It was time to head out. I heard Mrs. Miller say something about the next time adding my name, Rachel Lynn, but not really registering.

That was my cue, and I was out of there. My late-model Toyota was it for me. Getting into my safe haven, I let out a breath, started my car, and got a couple of miles away from her. I started watching the video again the moment I got out of the eyesight of the Miller home. I rewound the video to the beginning again and watched it carefully. He lay there with his eyes open, but no one was home. However, his penis was erect. This was curious, a drug that produced this result first? Then another that made him want to rape? He has many faults, but forcing himself on women is not in his nature. I turned the volume up to listen carefully. The Cat bitch climbed on my man and inserted him inside her. Then, just as she started rocking, I saw it again. The freaking tail. It was slowly rising with her orgasm and then went dead straight as she screamed out. Shane also screamed, making no other sounds. He never made that sound with me. It was more a growl and roar than a scream like men normally make. He lay back on the bed as she rolled off of him, uttering nonsense. Then he suddenly seemed to snap out of his catatonic state, looked at her, and turned to get out. That is when I could hear for a moment a hissing sound. He seemed to freeze in place. I suspect some kind of inhaled drug. He then attacked her. I am aware they sell these rape videos online. I suspect the con goes two ways. The first con is for the girl to get a mark to sign away the eggs for sale. She gets the rape videos for her to sell. Now I am pissed off again, just as the video ended. We are going to have to make love and have a baby and put that woman's scheming behind us. Jumping out of the car, I ran in place for a few minutes, psyching myself up. Yes, I can do this. I have a plan. Ok, now I'm done for the day and going home, but first, I need a little extra something for tonight.

When I heard the door open, I finished up my outfit by slipping on my shoes and bunny ears.

Shane's voice came from the living room, "Jack, you will not believe what Mr. Watkins asked me about when I showed him his...." The coat that he was taking off fell to the floor, and his mouth remained open when he saw me.

I hopped up to him, wearing the most revealing bunnies costume I could get on short notice. If he likes animals, that is what he will get, as long as it is from me only. I wrapped my right hand around his neck and pulled him in for a deep kiss. I undid his pants with my left hand and stroked him with my right. He offered no resistance as his hands roamed my hips, then my ass. I pulled back and asked, "So you like?" He pulled my head back to him, so he could reach my lips while groaning something unintelligible. I stepped back and turned around, so he could see my bunny's tail. Then I shook it, taunting him.

He grabbed it and pulled it to him. "You know, I find what you wear or don't wear sexy and irresistible. I will never stop wanting you. Tell me what this is about?" I grabbed his hand and pulled him to the bedroom, adding a lot of sway to my hips.

"Next week I'm fertile. We will have to have so much sex it may not be as much fun. We will have to find each other as soon as my body temperature is just right. I just want a little fun first."

He stopped, looking worried. "Jack, I love you, and I've always done what you wanted since we were kids. Why would you think you have to tell me the plan now? You chose me to be your husband/lieutenant, and I love you. I must admit, I love this costume, and I wouldn't mind if you wore it again." He was talking while kissing my neck and pulling me on top of him. "You know I love your body how it is naturally. I don't need incentives and attraction to another woman. Since the day you told me I was your man always. You said you forgive me. I don't even remember most of what was on the video."

After our conversation, we made love and despite my best efforts, he never made that sound for me, much to my disappointment. I wasn't angry at Shane, not really, but I felt I had something to prove. She was no better than me at controlling my man.

Chapter 2
Year 2026: Sweet Revenge

My temperature is right, according to what my AI says, and the calendar indicates I'm ovulating. I'm so excited. I rushed out the door with my supplies and quickly made up the SUV. Using the back with bedding, I added a blanket and pillows. Humming to myself, I laid out my clean-up clothes. Struggling out of my jeans by laying on my back in the vehicle. While twisting my butt to get out of my clothes, I found myself staring at the inside roof of the vehicle.

My mind sight went to envision myself holding a baby, counting his/her little fingers and toes. Smiling as I thought, *I'm sure I will get pregnant right away, if not this week, surely the next.* The child would have Shane's smile and caring nature but my strength and determination.

Getting back behind the wheel, I drove to where Shane agreed to meet me. I pulled up to our agreed location, and there he was, waiting, just like when we were in Foster care, always waiting when I told him to be somewhere. His firm jaw, kind eyes, and calm smile secured my esteem. He has never known how much I needed him, and I keep it that way. Even as a teen, he had well-developed muscles and was taller and stronger-willed than most other young men.

It didn't take me long to make him part of my gang of kids. Waving at him to come to me, he obeyed, as always.

Before we got to the back of the car, I pressed my lips to his and kissed him while I began unbuckling his pants. My hands scrambled to open the back door so that we could crawl back there. Fumbling like we were kids hiding from the police again, butterflies leaped in my belly as we both heaved ourselves inside. I called for the windows to darken and with the bedding, it was easy and the familiar smells of our home made it perfect. Shane groaned and panted as he pushed himself into me, first slowly, then faster, until we climaxed at the same time. Then I felt him do something unusual for him. Shane slowly pulled out of me, then put his fingers over my vagina to hold in his sperm. His eyes raised up to mine, saying, "I want a child with you as well." Funny, I thought. I never thought to ask him if he wanted this now. Then he kissed me gently. This time, now, some frantic passion changed to tenderness.

After six weeks of no success, frustration and anxiety were setting in with both of us. Shane was trying not to show it, but the spontaneity and fun had worn off. Now our meeting became more of a job, and I was losing hope.

I knew I needed help, so I made a video appointment with an Obstetrics doctor. I asked my doctor for fertility drugs and any other pointers to help us conceive. We put every one of his suggestions to use. Shane and I continued our clandestine meetings for several more months with no success. Finally, I made an in-person appointment for a full exam to find out what the problem was.

When I walked through the building doors, I thought there must be an issue with the reversal contraceptive drug. Maybe I didn't inject myself correctly, so I didn't receive enough medication. All they have to do is measure how much is in my bloodstream and give me the appropriate dose. Yes, that baby will be in my arms by the end of the year.

Hair stood on the back of my neck when the doctor asked to see me in his office after the tests. I was expecting a prescription to be sent to my pharmacy and the new medication to be waiting for me at home. When I entered, he asked me to sit while the look in his eyes increased my apprehension. I started to get up and leave the room right then. I knew he would say something I didn't want to hear.

The news was devastating. I could hardly keep my emotions in check in the office. The doctor said, "Rachel, your eggs are no longer viable. You are in early menopause." His sympathetic eyes scanned my face, trying to anticipate my reaction to his news as he spoke. "You can use eggs from a donor... blah, blah, blah."

I drowned the rest of what he said as the blood in my ears created pressure. My heart was trying to jump out of my chest, and red was encroaching on my vision. My skin was heating, and I was on the verge of exploding with my skin too tight. Without a word, I picked up my purse and walked out. Vaguely, I heard someone calling my name, but that was like a dream. I had murder on the brain, but it won't be quick. I'm going to find that Cat Bitch and make her life miserable for as long as I can. She messed with the wrong woman. There is a reason people call me Jack, and she will learn the hard way why.

As soon as I got to the car, the research began. Consulting my AI, I asked, "Brenda, open holograph images. Now show me all the colleges within a 20-mile radius of my home." The graph is populated with three red dots. Ok, I thought, I'm getting somewhere. "Now pull up videos 'College students rape videos.'" Using the face, I circled with my finger, searching the registry of the registered students for a match." I waited while the search bar circled, showing she was processing my request. She came back with no results. *Ok,* I thought. "Brenda, Search social media for matching faces with parameters. The first parameter is between the ages of 20 and 25. Second is approximately 5-0 to 5-3 and 100 to 120 lbs. Third, a trans-species person, a species cat within the radius. Start a search." My temper had cooled some, so I started the car and pointed the car home. When she said she had 15 people for review, I was about ten minutes from home. Now I was focused. I waited till I got home to even look. I was on a mission and took the time to prepare dinner first. Following that, I cast the pictures and media to the screen.

I had just gotten to the third person when Shane came in. He put away his tool bag and clothing, then walked to me, looking at the screens curiously. He looked at the screen, then back at me, waiting for an explanation.

"Shane, the doctor said it is too late for me to become pregnant naturally," I said this while not taking my eyes off the screen as I scrolled to the fourth candidate. Then I remembered he had a stake in this, so I glanced up at him, and he looked crushed. Wow, I didn't think it was that important to him. I sometimes forget how deep his feelings are. I said, "I have a plan. Not only that, I'm going to make that bitch tell me who she sold my eggs to and get them back. First, I'm going to torment her just as soon as I find her. Then she will run to her handler. From there, I will find my eggs, so we can have our baby."

He asked, "Do you think we can get them back?" The hope in his voice made me look up into his eyes, and the hope I saw there overwhelmed me. I stood up and wrapped my arms around him. I just was only going for the hug. He had other thoughts because he turned my head to meet his lips, then his tongue was in my mouth. It is so rare for him to start a kiss. We both acknowledge I'm the boss, making me the start of most things. I responded in kind to his kiss.

He finally pulled back and said, "I want to help. Once we find her, then we stake her place out and find her routine, then it is on."

Number eight was a winner. There was the Cat Bitch in all her feline glory. Her name is Jessica Lynn Lee. She is a licensed prostitute, which meant her contact information was available to the public. They did not post her address. However, back, tracing a few things from her advertising, I narrowed down her neighborhood to a two-block radius. That was enough for tonight, so we ate dinner and discussed our plan for the stakeout.

We began our search for her residence the next day. In between our clients, we could locate her building and apartment. It took about two weeks. Now stakeouts. We spent months learning routines because we couldn't consistently watch; after all, we also had to work. We spent a good amount of time watching her place while spending several nights in the car together. We took turns napping in the back. It was actually kind of fun for me, the closest I had come to camping for fun. Shane seemed to enjoy the closeness as well.

It's been a long time since Shane, and I committed a break-in together. After we finished Trade School, we swore we would be legit. Sure, we committed petty thefts to pay our way through school, but what else could we do? Our foster parents were kind enough to put up with me for the last four years of my time before I aged out. Shane was actually easygoing and untainted, but he did have some decent hacking skills. I was a very eager student to learn these and found ways to put these skills to use for our financial gain. As it turned out, we didn't need to hack the scanner on Jessie's apartment door. It actually had the old-fashioned key lock system. Fortunately, Shane and I were well-trained in picking the typical locks of this type. We even had a specialized set of lock-picking tools.

The home where we met was Shane's only foster home, but not mine. Our foster parent probably would have adopted him if I hadn't chosen him to be mine and corrupted his value system with my own.

"Jack, do we need the compressed air or not?" I heard him call out from the office.

"Yeah, I think so. Did you put the kitty litter in the car already?" I yelled back.

He was hauling another bag out of the office. "Yeah, I got it all loaded, and we are ready."

I was giddy like my first heist. The Cat Bitch won't know what hit her, I thought. Then we were off. We had calculated she would be out all night, but there was a contingency plan. We strategically placed Shane's AI on my car as a camera. It has her image programmed and would notify me if she was spotted. To break in her place was child's play for us. I cased her place carefully. The living room was quite large and furnished with a real wood table, soft plush chairs, loads of paintings and vases with fresh flowers. Quite tasteful, something I know nothing about but secretly admire. I barely resisted the urge to break things, which would tip her off too early. We walked into the bedroom together. I gasped. The bed was enormous. It had to be a California King, something I heard of but had never seen. This obviously is not where the videos are shot, but I didn't think she would be that stupid. The bed had loads of pillows decorated with gold, pink, black, and cat tails. Everywhere cats. Light shades, blankets, drapes, even cattails in vases. It was creepy. Picking up the black comforter splashed with white cats over it, I pulled it to my nose to get a sniff. The fragrance was difficult for me to place, maybe floral, but something else as well. Shane had wandered more in the dresser's direction to examine the contents on top. I was feeling the quality of the sheets out of curiosity more than working on our scheme.

From out of nowhere, I heard the same sound Shane made on the video come from behind me. He was holding a spray bottle that he apparently had squeezed, or maybe it was on some weird trigger. His back was to me, but I could see him in the mirror's reflection, and his eyes had glazed over. He looked like a zombie. I was so intrigued that he found the drug that I dismissed his condition. I knew he had the drug she must have used on him, and I wanted to get a better look at it. At that moment, it was the only thing on my mind. I dashed over, pushed past his prone stance, and took the bottle out of his hand. I brought it close to my face to further examine it when he grasped my waist. He pulled my yoga pants down forcefully and forced me over the dresser. My hands landed roughly on the dresser in front of me. Barely, I might add.

"What the hell, Shane? What are you doing?" I growled out just before I heard his zipper come down, and he entered my anus hard. I wasn't prepared, and it hurt. "Stop, Shane, Shane," I cried from the force of his forward thrust and pull. Finally, he made a high keening sound like a wounded animal (that I never want to hear again) upon his release.

Shane stumbled back afterward and fell to the floor, sitting up, looking forward, but with a blank look. I gathered myself and turned to look at him. He was sitting up, his eyes were open, and he had a color-drawn face, but there was no one home.

Kneeling down to him, I slapped his cheeks. "Shane, Shane, come back to me," I kept saying, with no response. Glancing around the room looking for a solution, my eyes stopped at the black and white door to the room, with the cat tails painted on. Jumping up from the floor, I went to the kitchen and got a cup of water. After retrieving the white coffee cup with the words "Catnip" printed on it, I filled it with water from the faucet. Putting my hand in the water to gather the wet drops, pulled it out and began flicking water in his face. The second time his eyes blinked, his lips began moving with no sound coming out, and color started returning to his cheeks.

Suddenly, tears began leaking out of his eyes. He let out a loud cry, "I'm so, so sorry!" His eyes remained fixed on me, and he cried. "Rachel, I messed up again. I hurt you. You won't want me anymore. Please don't leave me." Slobbering, he reached out for me while saying, "I couldn't stop myself. I don't know how it happened. I was there, but in the backseat, and couldn't stop."

Grabbing his face as I moved into his embrace, I kissed him. "It's ok. It was the drug. You didn't hurt me, and I still want you."

I lied about the pain. It hurt like hell, and I know I was bleeding, but he will never know. Whatever is in that stuff is dangerous; I will dump it and fill it with water. The next man won't rape her for her film. He will just get up and leave. I know she will probably get more from wherever such people cook stuff up like this, but at least it will save one guy.

He seemed satisfied that we were still together, wiped at his face and pulled himself together. As he stood, I could see the regret in every part of his movements. Knowing this man like I do, it was best to resume what we were doing and not mention what happened. We went on Project Gaslight The Cat Bitch, after I got Shane back together. I made a point of copying the information off her computer. She is working for someone. I want to know who. This will go a long way to fulfilling my plan to regain my property. We finished up after leaving our cameras and bugs.

Shane and I had plenty of laughs, watching the videos recorded from the cameras in her apartment. It was almost like a comedy hour watching her in some ways. That was only us softening her up for the actual game. We watched when she came home and got undressed to take a shower. I couldn't help but do a quick mental comparison between her figure and my own. The Cat Bitch is about 4 '11 or 5 '0 with small curves and hips, very small breasts and a flat rear end. I found with the mixed Asian features in her face made the cat-like features stand out spectacularly, especially complemented by the surgical cat-like optical enhancements.

In comparison, I am tall, about 5'9, lean with soft curves, a pronounced ass and high but small breasts. I like to think, with my cocoa brown skin, I resemble so many of the athletes breaking all kinds of records today. She came out of the bathroom with a towel around her head, bopping to some tune in her head. She went to open her top dresser drawer and moved around her panties, and barely avoided the snapping mousetraps.

Her screams as she jumped while jerking her hand back were music to my ears. It was only one trap, so she was ok, but she didn't go in that drawer again. She sat on her bed for a moment, then stood and opened another drawer. Nothing happened, so she pulled out a satin-type nightgown. I hoped that would be the one I sprayed the cleaner on.

On clothes, I find it makes me itch after a while. I use gloves when using them. She took the towel off her head, and a lot of her hair came out with it. Thanks to my hair removal additives in her shampoo. She initially didn't notice until she ran the brush through her scalp, and long strands of black hair fell in her face. She began screaming. Miss Jessie was in full panic.

I laughed so hard I barely heard when she spoke to her Temple Link Device. Practically screaming in her AI, saying, "Teddy, call Sandy." Now we are getting somewhere, I thought. She sobbed in between words, "Sandy, you got to come over here." She dissolved into sobs again, "Somebody's been in my apartment, and they trying to hurt me or something. Please just come over here."

Sandy replied, "Jessie, what do you mean somebody's trying to hurt you?" Sandy's voice was a husky, smooth voice. It sounded like she had a minor concern but was indulgent with her. Jessie continued crying, "They put a mousetrap in my drawer, and my hair is falling out! You promised! No one would come after me. That's the only reason I came to this crappy town!" She fell back on her bed spread eagle style, crying loudly. I even felt a little pity for her, but that's when she jumped up screaming. She just found the other mousetraps! The trap actually snapped one of the remaining strands of her hair. Dangling there like forgotten hair rollers while she jumped about the rooms crying, screaming, and snot running out of her whiskered face was hilarious. It was so hilarious, I fell out of my chair laughing so hard. She screamed like someone was stabbing her, ran for the door, grabbed a jacket out of the closet in the front room and headed out the door buck naked. She had just got the jacket on when the can of compressed paint sprayed her face a bright shade of crimson red. Screaming, she looked like a human-sized cat in a fight running down the hall, stumbling over her slippered feet. "I just can't handle this. I'm leaving here," said Jessie in a squeaky baby voice.

"Pull yourself together, girl. Why don't you just come over here, and we'll talk about it." Sandy answered. That was all we got before she went out of the range of our planted microphones. I was barely able to get myself off the floor and get reseated, so I laughed so hard. "Shane." I said in between fits of laughter, "The paint in the closet was a great idea. I didn't understand why you wanted to bring our pink concoction and spray it all over, but that worked out well." Jumping up from my chair, I sprinkled his face with kisses while embracing him in a hug. "We know everything that she touched in the apartment. We got her now. Likewise, we have her hand prints on everything. We can track back where she goes and the things she touches. Once she gets in the car, the AI you dropped in there will tell us where she goes. Whenever she goes, we'll know where she went and what she picked up while she was there. We have the drugs she used on you to make you crazy enough to rape. I'm not sure when or what we will do with it. Now, if we had enough to go to the apartment, hotel, or wherever she took you, this could work. Our knowledge of where the videos made after the drugs are used to make you all 'rapey' can blackmail her."

I looked at Shane, and he was looking at me with all the regret on his face. Grabbing his hand, I sincerely said, "Don't worry, Shane, I don't blame you for any of this. You know, as a matter of fact, I sprayed a bit of the drug on myself, and it gave me a sexual jolt. It didn't affect me the way it affected you, so I believe we tie it to something in men. We both know you have a lot of testosterone," and I gave him a smile. That made him turn up his lips a little, anyway. I believe that's all part of her and whomever she is working with's con. They weaken the marked men with a drug after she distracts them with her presence. Then they probably get him to walk to the room and get into the bed himself. They drugged the men with this spray and had what appears to be enforceable sex with her. She videotapes for her sick customers, then she can still sign away their partner's eggs. However, what I don't understand is why they need the eggs so badly. Who is in charge, as obviously this Jessie girl is just a minor player? We need to find the big fish and know where the eggs are sent. I plan on fighting so I can get mine back.

Shane and I continued watching the video we picked up from traffic cams. She drove to a large gated community with an entrance gate equipped with a code to enter. However, for the secondary entrance to the home, we wanted to include state-of-the-art drone hovering and optical verification scans, which she completed quickly as she proceeded up the drive. Now Shane and I knew what to do. We had to get in our car, find the community, and set up surveillance. After arriving at the gated community, we sprayed orange spray to find it easy to punch in the code. We did not enter the second entrance. We just wanted to know the code in case we use that avenue to get in. We now know the location of her handler, and it won't take long to find the owner's full name. Now the not-so-fun work will begin, the surveillance to find the vulnerable points to gain entry. My only regret at this point is that Jessie didn't find nearly half of the little goodies that we left for a special little kitty. At some point, she has to come back, or I will get my revenge at another time. This reminds me of old times, and I smiled to myself. As a teen, I never put much time into studying anything academic, unlike Shane. He already had some hacking skills. I found this particularly useful for petty theft. With some female encouragement, he not only taught me but increased his skills to almost an art.

Finding a little time at home, I plugged in the storage device I used to extract the files from Jessie's computer. It was worse than I thought. She had over a hundred rape recordings of staring at herself and various men. After scanning through about six or seven, I learned the play. It was similar to her assault on Shane. Initially, she would spray them with one of the concoctions I took from her house. This one made the victim docile. Next, I moved on to the bank accounts. The con job has been quite lucrative for her. There wasn't much more use of the drive, just her solicitation adds for her prostitution business.

Shane called out! "Jack,"

He stood behind me, shuffling his feet behind me. He only does that when he is unsure. I turned my head to look at him expectantly.

When did the smile drop from his face and be replaced with a frown? For a moment, I saw that fourteen-year-old boy I first met at Mrs. Miller's Foster Home. He knew what it felt like to be loved, and I wanted that. I couldn't tell him that, so I gave him such a hard time in the beginning. I wanted him to feel as unloved as I did. Later, I used it and offered him a chance to be my lieutenant in my gang. I put him and another young man through my version of a trial. It is composed mostly of various crimes. Shane was always the one I wanted, but my pride couldn't let him know that.

"Well, Shane, what is it?" I made sure he saw my irritation. That didn't really exist.

"Never mind," he murmured, turning around to walk away. I grabbed his arm, and, more gently, I pleaded, "Please say it?"

He stopped fidgeting and had the strangest look on his face, like a longing for something that I never bothered to ask. This was the moment in my adult life that my choice would profoundly change multiple lives. If only I had known that then if I only cared or let myself feel enough to care.

Shane blurted out, "We should let all of this go and continue with the life we have as it is. I like our lives without children." I think he even surprised himself with his candor.

A brief thought entered my head he was always a better person than I. His life after he came into foster care, may have been better for him before I corrupted him. He had loving grandparents that raised him from infancy. His drugged-out mother abandoned him in the hospital, and she couldn't remember who his father was. However, she returned to him when he was fourteen. He let her into his grandparent's house, and she killed them in their beds before killing herself. She never uttered a word of why. She just walked past him with a gun and did the deed.

Standing in front of me, looking at me with wonder, he watched and waited for my response. I said, "I thought you wanted what I wanted." I stood, wrapped my arms around him, and kissed him. As usual, he responded, and I got my way again. I am only six months younger than he is, but I don't have feelings, just needs. I said, "So we both go to our appointments as usual tomorrow. Since I am closer, I will do a little surveillance on the property of Sandy. I will probably be home just after you, so you can pick up dinner." I said this while kissing his ear lobe and rubbing his manhood. He groaned and shook his head in acknowledgement. I am the first woman he had ever been with, and until that bitch Jessie interfered, the only woman. She will get hers as I slowly "Hi Jack" her life, this part I won't tell Shane about. Shane believes they nicknamed me Jack at the foster homes. But the truth is when my rescuers found me as a traumatized child at four or five. That was the only name I knew. A DNA search found my birth name and my parents, but they had disappeared. I couldn't remember their names or faces. I only remember various foster homes.

Grabbing Shane by the hand, I led him to our bedroom, so I could kiss and suck away all his doubts. In the back of my head, I know I am wrong, using sex to have my way. Not ever knowing my parents or a functional relationship is my excuse. I know he is more than a blow-up doll and not here for my satisfaction. Shane just groans in pleasure and gives as good as he gets sexually. While I give in to his ministrations, I wonder if when I find my eggs and have a child, Shane will be able to give me all his love as he does now. Will I be jealous of my own child? I like to think not. Shane and I fell asleep entwined in each dirty and naked in each other's arms.

Chapter 3
Dark Proposal

I got to Mr. Mann's home a little early. Hoping to finish up soon, so I could take some pictures of Sandy's place at a decent time. I knocked, received no answer, as usual, inputted the code, and entered. Mr. Mann failed to answer. That was again not unusual, I headed for the basement, and he was not in there. He wasn't in the kitchen or the living room. I was really worrying. The man never leaves his home, absolutely never. I went to his bedroom and there he was, laying in the bed. Wow, still this time of day, how unlike him.

"Mr. Mann, Mr. Mann," I gently shook him as I called out. He didn't respond and wasn't wearing his AI. His face looked pale and even a little blue, his eyes were closed, and he was still wearing pajamas. I grabbed his cold and clammy wrist. Checking his pulse, I found, and it was weak and thready. My concern ratcheted up, and I knew it was time to call in experts.

Speaking to my AI, I called, "Brenda, please send emergency services to this address. Mr. Henry Mann is unresponsive. Please use my current location." She responded, "Acknowledged, services dispatched." As I waited by his bedside, a calm came over me. If I ever had a father, I would have thought he may have been like this man. Not the warm, cuddly type, but rough around the edges and caring. He told me how he always gave people a hard time finding out what made them tick. Most left him in anger, but I fit his personality. Smiling to myself as I remembered the conversation. That was the most I ever got out of him about his feelings. We probably argued more than ever got along, but that's how we worked. Fifteen minutes later, the ambulance arrived while I waited outside the door to wave them down.

Two EMTs emerged, pushing a gurney between them. One was a tall, rather thin white woman and the other was a young black woman around twenty or so. She appeared a few months pregnant. Staring at her slightly protruding belly for a moment, I forgot what I was waiting outside for. My first thoughts were how jealous I was for her to be pregnant and not me. My next thought was that since the onset of the vape drug O, the normal childbearing of her age stopped having children. How unusual is it to see a young Black woman pregnant? Without thinking, I let the two women by me to enter the narrow corridor. The gurney struggled around his clutter, bumping into and knocking over stacks. I quickly dove in between some stacks, aiming to position myself ahead of them. Now, preceding them, I guided them as effectively as I could, eventually, they got to him. They worked on him for a few minutes, then loaded him up on the gurney, and they were gone. Well, with nothing to do for the next three hours, I headed toward Sandy's house.

I got about five miles away, and who did I spot coming out of a convenience store? The Cat Bitch herself? Wow, something to brighten this sour day, I thought. I easily followed her. She was hard to miss. I guess she got over her fright at what Shane and I did. Because she was walking confidently on the sidewalk. She wore a skintight black leather top that only stretched to her abdomen. Black leather pants that had a large opening cut out to display her swinging tail and butt crack bottomed off with black high-heeled pumps with laces that went up each of her legs completed the outfit. What an ensemble, I thought. I watched her stride down the walk, swinging her tail attached to her small butt and narrow hips. She entered a Starbucks. Parking a few cars down, I got out. Walking right up to the outside of the door of the coffee shop, I waited. She eventually came out with four coffees in a paper carton in one hand and a bag of goodies in another.

I followed her as she approached a small red hybrid. Just as she was putting the coffee on the roof to open the door, I yelled in her ear, "Hey PUSSY, PUSSY, PUSSY!" She jumped about a foot in the air and screamed in fear. All the coffee flipped up in the air, spilling on her, the car and the ground. I kept walking past poor little Jessie like it was an everyday occurrence. A big grin spread across my face as I heard the screeching sound she made when the liquid soaked through her clothes, reaching her skin. The coffee burned her skin. I was almost sorry, but she made such a tempting target, and that was a little more payback for what she has no doubt done to men with her scams. Melting into the crowd of passers-by, seemingly oblivious to her coffee-stained plight, I smiled to myself.

I went on to Sandy's estate and began taking pictures using a telescopic lens. Even though I had the code to get to the estate, I made no attempt yet. I wanted to get a better look at the second gate. As soon as I even drove close to the gate, all of my digital equipment died. I was lucky I wasn't driving an electric car, or I would probably have lost that. This woman must have some kind of damping equipment targeted at cars not registered for the property. There is no way I will get to her in her fortress. This will take some time and planning for another approach to get to Sandy.

After about an hour of taking pictures, I packed up and went off to visit my other day's clients. I found time in between clients to call and check on Mr. Mann. The nurse at the hospital told me he was in a coma. It looked like he fell. He probably thought nothing of it, but his brain bled and swelled. He went to sleep and slipped into a coma. If I hadn't come by and found him, he would have died within the next couple of hours. It is unclear if or when he will wake. With no family, they listed me as a contact person. I remember him asking me if he could list me when we started working together. I never thought he would use it.

Soon, done for the day, I went home. When I pulled up, the hairs on the back of my neck stood on end when I saw Shane outside waiting for me. His eyes were enormous and face flushed. I couldn't read his expression, and I panicked. That was something very unlike me to show Shane's weakness, so I pushed it back down. I got out of the car as nonchalantly as I could.

"Shane, how are you?" I was walking and talking to him. I reached him and kissed him on his cheek.

"Rachel." His voice was elevated and panicking. When he calls me Rachel, I know what he has to say is important. Taking in a breath and beginning again, he said, "Rachel, someone has been in our house. Glancing around, I looked for our pre-entry, silent alarms that eerily sat deactivated by intruders. Shane exclaimed, "I entered and sprayed the orange spray to find items touched. The only thing taken was your underwear." He opened his mouth to continue, but I cut him off.

"Well, some teenage boy broke in and went through my panty drawer." I smiled, "That doesn't seem like something to warrant that look on your face." A deep frown came over his face, and his eyes still had that look of fear in them. "What, Shane, spit it out." I all but shouted out as icy fingers began creeping up my skin.

He cleared his throat and continued, "Not your panty drawer, but your dirty laundry in the hamper. That's not all. They urinated on my clothes, on the dresser and in different parts of the house. I can even smell it out here, but I don't know where." Now that was creepy.

It was like he was marking me. "Who did you piss off, pardon the pun?" Shane asked.

Not used to being on the defense with him. I stuttered, "I, I, I, don't know." My brain to really thought about all the people I had contact with lately and came up empty. "Just Jess, I messed with her when I saw her today. That's it."

He said, "We need to move to a Beta site and set up a new home." It is so rare for him to give me orders. I was so taken aback that I just agreed. Since we never put permanent roots anywhere, we packed in about two hours and moved to our beta site. It was a house that had been on the market for years. From time to time, we would check on it and make sure we had easy access. Shane decided we would maintain our current clients for our income. The idea was to begin phasing them out soon. By next year, we would be in another state. We had an emergency fund stashed in overseas accounts under false names. Either of us can access them electronically, but it was no need to go there yet. Anything electronic carries a genuine risk of being accessed by anyone talented enough. We agreed we would slowly phase our presence out of existence in this state. Then use our saved funds to set up elsewhere, maybe out of the country.

The next few months went by, and Shane didn't seem eager to scale down his clients. Whenever I asked, he became irritated and found different ways to avoid the subject. Bringing up our moving became a source of a rare argument between us. My tactfully trying to suggest we leave was wearing thin. On one particular evening, we sat and ate dinner. That evening, my mind was thinking again of leaving, but my husband's mind was far away. Shane was chewing his food and looked so deep in thought.

"Shane, what are you thinking about?" I asked him. I thought it would be some random thing, nothing deep, but he surprised me by saying.

"Jack, you know I think I would like to attend college to get a teaching degree. I would like to teach older children. I heard there are corporate schools being planned with a more rigid curriculum than the public ones we went to. They are developing the few children left after that Drug O that has almost wiped out the Black population and discouraged births in all races. There is a company here that will pay for my education. What do you think?" He looked so hopeful and positive.

I didn't know what to say. If he did, I couldn't follow. Maybe he would not need me. I just kept chewing and finally swallowed, forcing myself to answer. He waited patiently. Finally, I said, "Ok, let's look at the information together."

His smile could have brightened the sun. I don't think I have ever made him that happy. Wow, I thought, has everything always been about me? He is an incredibly easygoing man to the extent that I sometimes even forget that he is married to me. If I were capable of love, I would love him. For now, I just make him think I do. He seems satisfied with that. After dinner, he laid out his plan. He could attend classes online for the first two years. Life for us would continue as is for now.

It didn't, however, within a week, he was in the school. He had no time for me. All his time was spent on work and school. I came home from work but often left out again for hours. Feeling no guilt, simply indifference.

Leaving out the door, I would tell him it was to let him concentrate. It allowed me time to avoid explaining myself. I found myself back at, scouting out Sandy's place. Over the next six months, I tried to establish her pattern, a routine she performed. Once established, I would come up with a plan to retrieve my eggs.

Shane believed I dropped the matter, but I can't. That woman knew where my eggs were, and she would damn well tell me. Sandy never went to the same place at the same time and was with an elderly male. He was of average height, with white hair thinning around the outside of his head. I had no intention of questioning both of them, so I focused on Sandy's patterns. She was clever, typically taking different routes to various locations. She didn't even order food consistently at restaurants. It was so frustrating.

Finally, I found somewhat of a pattern. Her clothes! Watching her home as she entered and exited, it finally hit me. She favors skirt suits and pumps. They vary, but little. We are similar in height and weight, at least at a distance. I could wear a wig and glasses to impersonate her, and a plan formed. I had to order various colored skirts, blouse, jackets, and shoe combinations. Given that I wouldn't know in advance which outfit she intends to wear, I must ensure that I have multiple combinations readily available. I also need them to be easy to discard.

Finally, the day had come, and her usual male companion was not with her. I would strike at lunchtime. Parking a distance from her house, I observed her with binoculars. When she emerged from the house, I noted what she was wearing. A simple knee-length sky blue skirt and white blouse with ruffles. That combination, I had a close match for. The game is on. Following at a distance, we drove to a restaurant. I got out the matching set of clothes that were close enough to what she wore to fool people at first glance. After stuffing the ensemble into my purse, I waited. Her driver went to an upscale Chinese restaurant. That was perfect for my plans. I was wearing leggings, a tee shirt, a short jacket and shoes I could slip out of.

Taking a seat close to her, but not obvious, I watched as she ordered her tea. Opportunity struck. I stood and walked to the server, giving the pretense I was asking a question. Holding the menu up in front to hide the prying eyes of Sandy's men, I squirted a drug derivative in her cup.

The server was paying attention to the food item I was questioning and not my hand with the drug. Moments later, returning to my table, I ordered my food. Shortly after that, I patiently waited. I watched as her guards, who sat in booths nearby her, fixed their gazes mostly outside. The men determined I posed no threat and didn't bother to give me a second look. I got up after about fifteen minutes of my meal and went to the bathroom. Quickly

I reached into my bag and pulled out clothes very similar to what she wore, and changed into them.

A short time later, she came in. Just as she walked out of the stall, I sprayed on her with the same sedative Jess used on Shane. Not missing the irony, I congratulated myself on a well-laid plan. Shane and I both suspected Sandy was Jesse's source. The drug worked exceptionally. Her eyes glazed over before making her docile and cooperative. Removing the emotion from my voice, I instructed her to take a little nap. Since I had tested it out on my clients, I knew how long I had for her to be out, which was only minutes. Reaching into my bag, I slipped on the duplicate clothing and carried the bag on my shoulder. I hurriedly exited the bathroom and made my way back towards the kitchen. Making sure the guards got a glimpse of me was the tricky part. My heart pounded so loudly, I knew it would give me away. Pushing my jitters down, I hurried toward the back door when I saw the men rise from the table. Putting on some speed, I opened and shut the backdoor to mislead them but ducked into the pantry instead of going out of it. The plan was going off flawlessly so far. Changing back into clothes as quickly as possible, then stashing the clothes in my bag. Now the hardest part. This is that part that had the most chance of failure. I was hoping they would be delayed through my rouse.

Slipping back into the bathroom, I took several deep breaths. I got out of the syringe and held it to Sandy's neck. I smacked her face to wake her up. She moaned and drooled, then her eyes popped open.

A smile crooked her lips. "Jack, I presume." I had no time to learn how she could recognize me. She spoke in a hoarse voice, "After all those months of spying on me, you finally approached me. You know, you could have just come and knocked on the door. What would you like to do with me?" Still smiling and seemingly unbothered by being on the floor of a dirty bathroom, she waited for my response.

Her eyes roamed my face with total fascination and not fear. The butterflies in my stomach fluttered about. This only made me angry.

"Where are my eggs? Your minion tricked out of my husband. I groused out?"

She never stopped smiling, and her eyes spoke of joy as they continued to dance over my face. It was unnerving me. I almost dropped the needle and bolted for the door. My voice came out with more than the screech than I intended. "That's what this is about, well, sure. You know my boss will meet you soon."

That comment made my skin crawl. Hoping my inner feelings were not reflected in the tone of my bravado in my voice, "I don't care," I growled out.

Just tell me what I want to know. "Sure, anything," she said. The smile was still on her face while she looked at me like I was a fascinating bug under a microscope. Without delay, she began speaking to her AI, "Thomas, locate the embryos of Rachel Lynn Monroe, saying it out loud, for my sake." Thomas answered, "They are the property of Penelope Matthews in Maryland." Never having time to process the fact that she not only knew my face but my name.

The door burst open with a reverberating boom. Pissed off, guards were standing in the doorway. One of the men wore a black leather mask over his face. *That was strange*, I thought. *Either he didn't wear it out in the restaurant, or I didn't notice it.*

The angry look the two men gave me made my skin crawl. I stayed too long. Grabbing Sandy's head, I put the needle to her neck. "I'll kill her!" I yelled to the men. My voice coming out sounding a lot more confident than I was feeling. Both were tall, muscular men. One had a short bushy crop of black hair, an elongated face and a protruding jaw like a snout. All I could see were brown eyes, a long face, and thick lips despite the leather mask. The duo stood, blocking any escape through the doorway. The guards did something strange. They both visibly sniffed the air with their noses pointed toward the ceiling. The masked one turned from me to ask Sandy as though I was a minor inconvenience.

A deep, almost unnatural voice grunted out from the unmasked man, "What do you want us to do? She is his." Forgetting my position for a moment, I couldn't help but shoot out the question asked, "Say what, whose? What does that mean?"

They all ignored me. Sandy, still calm, responded, "Well, you have her scent, and you know she is not to be harmed. Let her go," they both backed away from the doorway. The two men looked angry but did as they were told. I brought Sandy up with me as I stood. We walked out to my car together. With my left hand, I reached for the door handle, giving her a little shove. I released her.

Sandy was breathing hard from the ordeal and pleaded, "Rachel, we won't hurt you. You can ask me anything you want. Just come to me and I will see you get it. This is totally unnecessary."

Confused and scared, I couldn't believe her, although part of me wanted to. I looked in the mirror, and even with me towering over her and a syringe at her throat, she stood there with that grin on her face. Even though I couldn't trust her, I couldn't help but be a little impressed with her. They made no move to follow me as I started the car. That was so creepy. I was thinking about what to tell Shane as I got in the car and went home. I kept quiet. Meanwhile, I will try to find out who this Penelope Matthews is and what did she do with my eggs.

A couple of days later, I left out to my clients. I still was no closer to locating the correct Penelope Matthews. Who knew there were so many in the state of Maryland? My next client favors a candy bar I pick up at the store. I get more progress out of him with it. After leaving the store, I walked past two men that were near the entrance, and I swear they both smelled me and smirked. That was so weird. Moving to the car as quickly as possible, I got in. *Raising my arms, I smelled myself; nope, I didn't forget my antiperspirant*, I thought. I checked my breath, it seemed fine. Maybe I should go back to the store and get some gum or cheap body spray. Opening the car door and placing one foot outside of it, I pulled it back inside when I caught a glimpse of the men. They were staring directly at me as though I was their favorite pork chop dinner. Even If I stink, it's better to find somewhere else to freshen up. Speaking to my AI, I instructed it to plot a course to my next client's home and the self-drive mode was engaged.

The rest of the day went as normal until I was on my way home. A truck came up behind me on a single-lane road, and another came from a side road to cut me off. The car was forced to engage the brakes, slamming my head back against the headrest. The brakes barely stopped the car in time not to hit them. The other truck pulled off and left just before I had time to react. While still sitting there, trying to gather my wits, this enormous man appeared at my car door. My mouth was left a gape when I realized it was the man in the leather mask, and he was grinning. He snatched open my door and pulled me out like I weighed nothing. He pinned me against the car and smelled me.

I started kicking and punching for all I was worth, which turned out not to be much.

He said in a deep voice, "You've met your match, he snarled out, Hi-Jack. This is not a situation you can hijack, he grunted. I'm going to make sure your life is as worthless as you are." He restrained me with his bulk as he looked at me with utter malice in his brown eyes that looked familiar, yet not. Then another man approaches. He must have been in the other truck.

The leather mask man released me and I fell to my hands and knees. The other man lifted me up in his arms with some reverence and continued to hold me in his arms like a lover. We finally meet Rachel. I'm Ricky. He did the same smelling thing, but more thoroughly, even throwing in a lick of my neck. His hard features made what could have been a handsome face more monstrous. He turned the both of us so that now his body was against the car. He wrapped his right arm over my chest, with his large meaty hand resting on my left breast. The other hand was over my crotch, which I am sure was no accident. He laughed in a deep rumbling sound. His voice sounded like a mouth that wasn't quite meant for speech. It was thick and words came out forced.

He continued with, "We finally see each other again. Well, it's sharing time. You have been on my radar for some time now. Even before you and Shane visited one of my little pussycat's home, incidentally, that was very distasteful to you too. You, too, worked to gaslight her." The man made a sound of sucking his teeth as if I was some misbehaving child. He whispered in my ear, "I must admit, the hair removal in the shampoo was really harsh." He swung his head back and forth and scrunched up his well, I guess, snout some. "So you and Shane are now living at that blue house at the end of the cul-de-sac on Robin Hill Road? You think you will stay there long enough for Shane to get his Teaching Degree?"

My heartbeat was pounding hard enough to be heard by this asshole. This guy knows too much, and I know nothing about him. I tried to calm myself. He could kill me anytime if he chose. "Who are you? What do you want from Shane and I?" I asked, using the most confident voice I could muster. He loosened his grip on my breast a little, but not enough for me to escape.

With amusement in his voice, he said, "I'm glad you asked. I have long-term plans for you." He smelled me again, then licked my neck. Repulsed but a little turned on, too. I tried to push that part of me as far down as I could.

"You know all of my men can smell you wherever you are and have been. As a matter of fact, you are fertile and are putting out some powerful pheromones." He moved his hips, so I could feel his enormous erection as he took another lick. This time I felt sick.

Being raped is not an experience I wish to repeat, and I'm not talking about Shane. I don't count what he did as rape. The drug The Cat Bitch used on men probably came from pheromones or at least where they produced it. Is it pheromones from human women? Is that possible? I wondered. But that is not my immediate problem, despite my revulsion. I was more turned on than ever, and I needed to escape. Groaning out, "Well, I got news for you, Asshole, I can't have children. There he got the wrong girl."

He laughed that demeaning laugh again, saying, "That's what the doctor said, and that is true. That man isn't the right man for you to conceive. However, the doc was to give you options. You are special and would produce exceptional offspring with the right partner."

He rubbed my breast and breathed into my ear. Ricky M shrugged and laughed. "Needing to observe you some more, I wanted to see if you had the fire and the passion I need."

I tried to pull away from him again. This time I caught him off guard. My knees buckled before I fell. However, Asshole caught me before I hit the ground. I regained control and stood back up.

"He is my husband, with or without children," I spat out.

"Well, for now, that is part of the deal I'm offering you. My name is Ricky M, and this is my territory. I know everything and everyone in it, and most work for me. I can use your talent for Gas Lighting people, but I don't need Shane. You don't love him anyway. You tolerate him out of some sense of feeling of power. You will be the power you were meant to be, and he will have the mundane life he should have always had. I am sure you are aware of the population decline here in the country. We all must do what we can to contribute."

Ricky M licked his thin lips as he stared at me with lust-filled eyes. "Your African American reproductive material is in high demand with the decrease in the black population. Think of the waste with you unable to produce with your soon-to-be ex-husband.

There is a mate waiting for you that will make use of those eggs and that body of yours." He eyed me like I was a large chocolate cake that he couldn't wait to dive into. Now my skin felt like it wanted to crawl off my body. His eyes appeared to be eating me whole as he continued, Shane and you have one week left in your marital bliss, then you divorce and come with me. Shane can be a teacher, find a woman that can love him and give him a true partner. You know you can never love or allow him to be a partner. You never knew how. I will give you the challenges you need without the emotional baggage. He released me, now run on home. Shane is there now, waiting for you. Give him your news and I will find you in a week." I just stood there in shock. With a smile on his face, he turned around and confidently swaggered off, heading towards his car, and smoothly drove away. I stood there and watched him leave, my mind racing a mile a minute.

Finally, I started thinking, what if they sent someone after Shane? I need to call and warn him. I turned toward my car and stopped.

Leather face man was still there, he was leaning against his truck with his arms folded. What now? I picked up my pace and ran to my car. Just as I reached out to grab the handle, his hand was there first. How could he have covered the distance that fast? There was no time to think about it before I felt the burn of a hard slap across my cheek. The ground was rising faster to meet me than my hands could brace. He caught the back of my shirt seconds before I ate the dirt and pulled me back to my feet. "You don't know how much I hate you. If others weren't in play, I would show you." He sneered this at me with the most malevolent look I had never received from anyone. "I will have to be satisfied with the fact that in a week, you get to watch Shane walk away from you to be happy in the arms of another woman. Not a broken thing like you." With those words, he opened my car door and shoved me in and turned to leave with unnatural speed. Within moments, he was at his truck. He saluted me, cracked a half grin, started the truck, and was gone.

Chapter 4
What have I done?

As I drove home, my burning cheek and my shattered self-worth were open for anybody to see. Feelings of shame and weakness seemed to be written on my forehead and reflected in the rearview mirror. This was all my fault because of my arrogance and impatience. I unleashed a crazy man on my husband because I couldn't let things go. Now he may be hurt, bleeding or at worst dead. Shane, my only real thing in the world, deserved better from the world. In my past, beating, starvation, and rape chased me, but I gave as good as I got. My dignity remained because I protected Shane from those horrors. Even building a semblance of arrogance around me, I believed I had punched the worst of what life had to offer in the nose. Ricky M and Leather Face were trying to tear my world down and destroy Shane in the process. That Leather faced man's words stung like a blow to my face.

My brain was in a fog as I pulled into my driveway. I tried to push myself-loathing away. The feelings filled me with so much indecision. Do I love Shane? Do I drag him into my problems once more? If I don't love him, then I could force him to once again be my champion, fight back and solve my problems. I never thought I loved him. I'm not capable of that emotion, but I have grown so used to him. If there was anyone in the world that I would love if capable, it would be him. He is so deserving of a much better person than me, maybe he should take Ricky M's offer. I walked into the house and a small pool of blood was on the floor. All indecision left as panic seized me. I think my heart stopped beating. I followed the drops to the bathroom in a zombie-like state. They have already killed Shane. I'm too late, my eyes filled with tears on the brim of dropping to my stinging cheek. The door was closed while I heard the water running. Putting my hand out and touching the door, I slowly pushed it open.

Expecting to see Shane lying dead on the floor, the sight in front of me was so unexpected that the tears slid and dripped out of my eyes. Instead, I heard him yell, "Oh, you scared me; why did you open the door so creepily?" Shane never looked up as he was spraying water over his injured hand.

I let out a breath I didn't realize I was holding. I uttered out, "What... happened?"

He continued rinsing without turning his head and said, "Some idiot ran into me at a stoplight a few minutes ago. It wasn't hard enough to deploy the airbags, but then he just sped off. Well, when I got home, I ran my hand along the bumper to check the damage and cut myself on this thing, a strange piece of metal." He picked it up from the sink and held it out for my inspection. Still not looking at me, he was staring at the odd technology, "I'm not sure, but I think it is some sort of tracking device. It has no electrical charge that I can detect. Once I bandage my hand, I will check your vehicle for one." His eyes drifted to mine to gauge my reaction to his information. He didn't initially notice my damp burning cheeks, and I decided I wouldn't tell him about Leather Face.

The floodgates of years of pent-up emotions I didn't think existed came flooding out. Tears welled up and rolled uncontrollably down my cheeks. Shane looked at me in total shock. He had never seen me lose control before, let alone cry, in all these years. It just hit me that my selfishness has put such a good man in danger. If I was just satisfied with what I had, all would be well. I must be the one to sacrifice this time, not him. Letting the tears and snot flow and through them, I confessed for the first time, "Trapped and abandoned in a jewelry store at age five and left for dead was my first memory. I only remember flashes of arms holding me in an air shaft.

Then falling and hitting the ground hard. The rest of the story is only what I was told by caseworkers." I couldn't look at Shane's face.

On some level, I realize he never saw the confession coming. A torrent of words tumbled out, and there was no closing the barn door now. "My parents were thieves and con artists with several arrests each, which had me to get into small places. The job went sour. They ran and left me. Since they were still outside when I fell, they got away. Remaining in the shaft compartment of the vent, my rescuers told me I'd spent days in there, and I blocked out most of it. Mostly dead when found, I spent months in a hospital. I don't remember if I was conscious any of the time there or not.

Still crying now more loudly. "My DNA has unknown and illegal enhancements" I doubt if he could understand me anymore as I cried and just couldn't pull myself together. Meanwhile, Shane just waited patiently for me to exhaust myself. "My parents did things to me before I was born so that they could have the perfect little tool." Letting all this out felt good and was quite unintended when I came home.

Examining Shane's face as I slowly emerged from my memories. He pulled me down to sit beside him. We both sat on the floor of the bathroom, now in silence. Shane's arms wrapped around me, providing me with the comfort I accepted but didn't deserve.

Looking into his pained-filled face and continuing. "I didn't know my parents' real names or their addresses. I only knew they called me Jack. Blowing air loudly out my nostrils, I continued, "My memories are so fuzzy." Leaning back against the wall, I began swiping the tears from my face. Sighing, "At least, that is what I was told. I don't think I even attended school before foster care. Anyway, I pretended it was a name the foster kids gave me, short for hijack. My parents never came for me, so the system passed me around in foster care."

Raising my head to look him into his eyes, I pressed on, "When I saw you at fourteen, already broken, I hurt you at first, not giving you the love in return. You should have turned to run at the first sight of me before I ruined you. Now I was so afraid I had gotten you killed. My life included beating, rapes and more many times than you could imagine, but no love until now." Rubbing my fingers over the cheeks of his beautiful face. "You, however, had been loved, and I wanted that. You were always better than me and could accomplish more. I realized at that moment that if I could make you need me, I would finally be able to experience love.

This is where he tried to hold me tighter. I wouldn't allow what I didn't deserve. I pushed him back. "No, I must tell you the truth. Now I have got myself into deep trouble, and you will not go down this rabbit hole with me. Do nothing, I don't deserve it. I have a price on my head. This insane rich man wants me, but not you. He may do right by you, or maybe not. In any case, I caused all of this, and I'm sorry. If I had only listened when you said walk away, I just couldn't and confronted Sandy on my own." Shane's eyes widened. He obviously had no idea but said nothing. Tears started again, "They will find me wherever I go. They already know way too much about me. I will not tell you much more for your own protection, but we have to leave now to get you away." Rising, then walking past him, I blew my nose and dried my tears. I felt like it lifted a weight off my chest. I thought *He needs to be free of the yoke that is me*. This is so much bigger than what we can handle. They said they would come to me in a week, but that was a lie. It will be sooner, probably in a couple of days. Today's accident was a show of power. Either I cooperate with whatever they want, or you pay the price. They want me to divorce you, and I think that may be for the best, to protect you. All of our investments will be in your name, take everything and have a real life." Tears wet my cheeks again. I didn't want to walk away from him. I certainly don't understand why I'm so emotional.

These kinds of feelings are not something I have. Blowing my nose, wiping my face, I spoke again. "Don't underestimate them." Through the entire conversation, Shane remained stoic and absorbed what I was saying. He took hold of my hand and guided me gently to our bed, where he pulled me onto his lap – a moment that, despite my years of struggling with control issues, I had never allowed to happen before.

Shane finally was able to speak, he asked in a choked-up voice, "I have always wondered if you love me since you have never said?" I sat on his lap, still sniffing, and buried my head in between his neck and shoulder and didn't have the courage to answer. I truly didn't know. He wrapped me in his arms and said, "Thank you for letting me see this side of you. I've often wondered what made you who you are. Then he kissed my sore cheek." I jumped in response to the sting on my cheek from his kiss, and he stared at the cheek. Rage entered Shane's eyes as he asked with clenched teeth, "Who hit you, Jack?" I looked down at my lap in shame, then returned my eyes to meet his. "I don't know, the man with Ricky M." Shane remained quiet for so long panic gripped me. What if he is the one that leaves me or goes after Ricky M's man? I thought. Instead, Shane caressed my face and said, "I want to show you how much I love you." My joy, because of his acceptance, was almost overwhelming yet unwise. His hands began to roam my body.

If I give myself over to my husband now, then I can release all the tension in my body. We have at least a couple of hours. Then I can make a clear-minded decision. I took off my clothing and began taking his off. At this moment of vulnerability, I needed Shane more than I have ever had. He was right there for me, as he has always been. My pride made me too blind, and I couldn't see before now. He was the one with the strength. It was never me. Then I pulled him in the most passionate kiss I have ever given. It felt like tons of rocks; the chip on my shoulder I carried was being carried by him. My husband.

Our lovemaking was slow. We didn't even stop to eat dinner. I felt complete and finished for the first time in my life, giving Shane all of me. We fell asleep, still naked, entwined in each other's arms.

A few blissful hours passed. The lights flipped on, blinding me. The hair on the back of my neck stood; I knew we were no longer alone in the room. My eyes shot open in time for a gloved hand to cover my mouth. The face of Ricky M leaned over my bed, staring at me. Swinging my head to look at Shane, my heart jumped into my throat. The Leather-faced man had a large knife to my husband's throat, and Shane's eyes looked to be bugging out of his face. Ricky removed his hand slowly while wearing a grin on his face. I sat up and swung my fist at his protruding jaw, which Ricky M easily ducked. Could this be the same Leather-faced man that was guarding Sandy? How many could there be? The same guy that backhanded me yesterday, I couldn't tell. There was no time to dwell on that, I needed to get us out of here. Damn, my weakness, I should have had Shane pack up and leave instead of blubbering all over him.

The grin remained on Ricky's face as he looked at Shane and said, "Hello, Shane, my name is Ricky. Jack here has been a busy beaver in my territory, and now she will become my new employee. The thing is, she needs to live with me and there is no room for you." Ricky M even pouted, like it was disappointing news.

Continuing dramatically, "Our interview process started when our Jessie played with you the night you two had intercourse the first time." Ricky M's lips turned up even more into a smile as he implied it was both consensual and multiple times. Ricky M pointed his fingers between us. Then we did a thorough background check on the both of you. This afternoon I made the job offer to the one I wanted. I'm here to clarify it. She has tonight to decide. Ricky M spoke as though this all was a done deal, the grin didn't leave his face.

"Come with me now, and you can sign for divorce electronically, and Shane can go on to his new wife. Look, we will help him be a teacher in one of my schools." While he spoke, his eyes roamed my naked body, and I didn't give him the satisfaction of covering up. I just stared at him back with contempt. Ricky M barely acknowledged Shane as he let the lust for me show on his face. The plastered-on grin slipped as he said, "Shane goes either way." Shane struggled, and the Leather faced man restrained my husband in a chokehold. Ricky M's head swung from me to Shane while wrapped up in the arms of his captor. He spoke with disdain as he addressed Shane.

"You can, of course, go on with your life without her, and I will even support your teaching effort." Ricky M treated Shane like something stuck on the bottom of his shoe. He looked at his leather-faced partner. "I am a generous guy, you know," and smiled. The Leather faced man's face never lost its sneer. Ricky grabbed both my hands in one of his and yanked me to my feet, then spun me in one swift move. My naked body was pinned against his fully dressed one, with my rear at his front. One hand held both my wrist behind my back, and his other hand squeezed my chin. So that now I was forced to look forward, looking into the horrified eyes of my husband. Ricky's hand left my chin and disappeared. Still looking at Shane, something changed. In Shane's eyes, the strongest look of rage I have ever seen. He looked as though he would chew through his captor if given one moment of chance. Never had I thought Shane had it in him to feel such anger. Guilt again fell over me like a curtain. I caused this. Before I could process it, the sound of Ricky M's hand was rummaging around in his pocket for something came to me. Shane's look held me in place, shock of rage on Shane's face froze me with indecision. His eyes widened, and he started struggling even more earnestly, trying to get to me.

I then felt the stab of a needle into my neck. Now I know why Shane had that look on his face. Speaking with joy in his voice, Ricky M said, "You like to run, right? Well, I will give you a chance to run and be faster and stronger than ever. Your increased pheromones are a problem if you aren't his match. He won't want you anymore." Demented Ricky made no sense, and I didn't care. Shane and I needed to get away now! The warmth from the drug spreading from my core and flooded my body. It wasn't unpleasant, just strange. Ricky licked my neck and groaned, all the while, he kept up his insane speech.

"You didn't get the full effect of my medicine yet. When we are together, that will change." He looked at my Shane, who was still being restrained by Leather Face, like he was a minor nuisance. In the corner of my eye, I caught a glimpse of another syringe coming out of one of Mr Crazy's pockets. Ricky M's hands moved from his cargo pants. I had barely enough time to register what was he doing when a sting, and then all lights went out. I forced my eyes open when I heard Shane screaming my name in a panic. Coming back to myself, and found I was laying face up on the bed, free from restraints. My head swung to Shane's voice, and he was still being restrained. The memory of what was happening came back to me with a start.

Shane was screaming, "Oh God, Thank God they didn't kill you." His eyes were only on me, and mine were following the Leather face man as he produced and aimed a syringe at Shane's neck.

Jumping off the bed, I launched myself at the leather face man to stop him from hurting my Shane. My thinking was fuzzy, and my limbs responded sluggishly. Leather face backhanded me on the other cheek. His strike tossed me back on the bed with enough force that I bounced off the bed only to flip face down on the floor.

Ricky M screamed, "You Moron, I told you before she is not to be hurt, she is too valuable. You hit her again, and I will kill you with my bare hands."

Shaking the cobwebs out of my head, I pushed myself to my feet again. In time to see Shane's eyes roll back in his head. Leaping over the bed, I was on him in time for him to slump in my arms to the floor. We all just stared at Shane, who lay on the floor motionless. I patted his face to wake him. "I am not going anywhere without him. Please wake up, Shane," I shouted. Shane's eyes opened, but that wasn't my husband in there. His pupils had turned beet red, and he made a growling mulling sound that didn't sound quite human. I stood and backed away. I was now standing against the wall and still very naked. It took both men to restrain Shane as he lunged for me with malice in his eyes. Shane was growling, and drool was running down his face.

Leather face looked at me with a sneer and said, "You had better run. He may have had a terrible reaction. He just might fuck you to death." Obviously, he wasn't unhappy with this turn of events.

Ricky M interrupted, "Something has gone wrong! We will handle this. You need to go!". Shane was insanely strong, like a man on PCP. The two of them could not restrain him for long. Ricky M's grin was finally gone, now replaced with panic. Ricky was obviously losing his grip, and Shane looked at me as though he were a rabid dog and I had stolen from him. Leather face, who I would guess barely restrained him, wasn't gripping any longer. Shane turned and bit Ricky M on the arm, jerking his head back and forth like it was a juicy bone. When Shane pulled back, there was skin and meat in his teeth. He chewed and gulped it down. Blood ran down to the floor, and someone screamed. I think maybe me. My head swung to Ricky M, hoping for this to be a normal thing. The man's eyes bulged with pure horror, and blood dripped from the newly-formed hole in his forearm. Ricky M shouted, "He was supposed to not want her, but he wants her more now. I don't know if he will help, kill or fuck her. Jack, you need to run, now!"

That was enough for me. I got up and ran out, naked as I was. Thinking fast, I grabbed my to-go pack underneath the porch. As I ran, I strapped it to my back. Under normal conditions, I can outrun Shane, but I don't know if I can in his current state. Moments later, pine needles were being crushed under my feet, and I was jumping over fallen logs. Brush and tree branches reached out to strike me in the face, and I was trying to reason out what just happened and where should I go. Moments later, the crashing of wood and clatter echoed throughout the woods. Then unintelligible screaming.

Shane and I chose this location partly because they backed it up to a wooded lot in case we may need it as a quick escape, and that is what I ran for. Knowing not to use trails, he knew as well as I, so I ran for the thick brush. I was still barefoot, but I had to ignore the pain. I would need at least five minutes to change into protective clothing, but I don't have it. The brush was crashing behind me quickly, close, way too close. Adrenaline was flooding my body. I need to keep moving and strategize. I don't have the time or strength to beat Shane in a contest of endurance. I have to out-think him. Not knowing if Ricky M or Leather-face is out there or not has to be put in the back of my mind, but I would have to assume so. I have a few weapons in my bag, but I don't want to hurt Shane. I don't give a damn about the other two. I would easily hurt them if given a chance.

The sound of breaking twigs and that odd mulling sound snapped my mind back to my immediate issue. I was still moving at a steady clip through the foliage, all the while strategizing. How is he tracking me? He is no boy scout, and I don't know if that drug gives those other freaks that sense of smell and strength. I could hear footsteps, breaking branches, and heavy breathing not far behind me. *Damn,* I thought *already*. I changed direction abruptly and went west to test my theory. I would guess if I stopped and stood still if he was using sound, he would stop and wait for me to move. If he stopped and changed direction with me, he was probably using smell. If that was the case, climbing a tree was out until I could throw off his sense of scent. I believe he is relying on a particular scent. Moments later, I could again hear him behind me. Ok, he is likely tracking me by smell. Now I started thinking. I know this is going to be gross, but it is all I could think to work with on the run. Picking up hands full of leaves, I used them to wipe under my arms, my vagina, and anus.

Scattering them around by tossing them in the air. Repeating everywhere I went as often as I could. I let the wind take the leaves with the scent of me all over. Then stopped and changed directions several times. After about a couple of miles of this, I found a climbable tree and scurrying up it. Scraping my arms and legs badly, I hoped I would have time to treat them soon before he figured out to follow a blood trail. I waited. Fifteen minutes went by and nothing. It looks like my ruse worked. I didn't come down; instead, as quietly and as delicately as possible, I put on my only change of clothes. My feet were so bruised that my pair of running shoes wouldn't fit. A small price to pay; I hope Shane is ok, but it's too dangerous to check yet. After an hour, I came down and started walking until I could find some shelter. In the first home I found, people were inside, however, the garage looked available.

My to-go bag held my favorite set of lock-picking tools, the same set I used to open the door of Jessie's apartment. Sneaking in by picking a lock, I found a place where I could see if anyone approached and to rest. I curled up beside an old, dismantled car and stained blankets on the ground and went to sleep. I never thought I would live on the street again, but one never forgets how. When the sun peeked through the dirty window hours later, I reached for Shane, who wasn't there. The memories of the night came flooding back, but it was no time to dwell. I suddenly realized I ran through those woods in the dark, only lit with moonlight, and I could see. What the hell did Ricky M do to me and Shane? I need to check on Shane to see if he was where I last saw him. First, never leave an area without taking advantage of usable items. I searched around the garage first to see if there was anything usable.

There was no food or clothing, but there was a first aid kit. I removed gauze bandages and antibacterial spray to put in my bag. Ignoring the pain in my wounded, now bandaged feet and swollen face, I crept out of the shed and ran back to the last place I saw Shane. He was not there, but there were a lot of disturbed leaves and drag marks. Since there were only small drops of blood, I assume he was unconscious, like when he sprayed himself at Jessie's place and someone dragged him off.

My heart ached. This is all my fault. I want him back. Did Ricky M kill him? Is he sick? Is he dying? Another thought hit me. Maybe he has found he no longer wants me like Ricky M suggested? If that is the case, I made promises to myself that if that is the case, I will not fight it. His happiness is important to me, I will find him or die trying. Looking around, I decided this was as good a place as any, so I propped myself against a tall tree. Pulling out my stolen first aid kit, I treated my myriad of scrapes, cuts, and bruises.

Chapter 5
At my wit's end

Making my way in a haze down the street, one that has several residences. I scanned the area looking for one that appeared vacant and had no visible alarm system or drones, especially since our home was out of the question. How did Ricky M and Sandy have so much information on me, I thought I was stealthy. Why me? These questions floated in my head as I wandered through neighborhoods. After several minutes of surveillance, my eyes landed on what I was looking for. I used my lock-picking tools and entered the residence. It was a decent three-bedroom rambler in between two other cookie-cutter homes. First, I needed clothes and food.

There were some yoga pants, a couple of shirts, socks, and no shoes that fit when I checked the closets and drawers. I checked for non-perishable foods that I could store first. I took some bags of tuna and other meats that I could open without tools. Locating soups and finding 'shakes to heat'. These are some of the most convenient foods. I have known I would have to be careful to take as little as possible so they are not likely to report the theft to the police. I took some wash towels, and soap, so I can wash at convenience stores if I have to. Now I've spent enough time here, probably about fifteen minutes, so I packed up and left. The soap and wash were unnecessary now and could wait. Now I need computer access.

After visiting another home that fit my skill set for burglary, I did the same thing. In addition to the food stores, I left the house with a tablet, intending to return the tablet, of which I later did. I walked out to the nearby park to use the internet to answer the question of who is Ricky M. A short search yielded answers. Ok, I said to myself, so his name is Ricardis Mathias Matthews. The soon-to-be-dead man is the owner of the leading Implants company. The organization specializes in animal implants and DNA injections. It is a global company with distribution to various subsidiaries.

Wait a minute, I started thinking. Didn't Sandy say that Penelope Matthews of Maryland had my eggs? Coincidence, the same last name? Who is she too, Ricky M? I did a Google search and found the connection. His 80 something year old aunt took my eggs last year? What, Why! She lives in Maryland and her son runs a large company as well. Penelope Matthew's son Clifford Matthews is also wrapped up in the campaigns encouraging women to carry children of all ages. Wow, these Matthew's men are really concerned with the population decline. Hmm, I said, that information is interesting and weird but irrelevant. I may do further dig on that later; the African and Native Americans are the hardest-hit ethnic group in the country. First, I need to find out where does Ricky M live? Is it a chance that Shane is still alive, and is he there? I have to believe he is and is unable to return to me.

Finally, while I have the tablet, I thought *I'd checked on Mr Mann to find out how he was doing. A few clicks later and sadly, I got my answer.* I found he had passed away. He once told me I was his only friend alive, and I didn't think until now to check on him. Guilt churned in my stomach. I hated being out of touch with him for so long, yet how could I know my life would take such a turn in the past twenty-four hours? Saddened by his death; it is a break for me. Heading to his home to use it as my temporary base was the plan. I thought I won't be on the streets tonight. Sourcing a bike, I pedaled my way over there in about three hours. Scoping out the house first, I found it seemed clear. I entered and began setting up booby traps and early warning signs. I also needed back doors for exits. It is nice to have a roof over my head for however, it lasts. Now I can continue my search for information with a full belly and relative safety. Since I had his access codes from my teaching him to use his systems, I also could use his bank accounts. I don't need them now, but maybe in the future. Everything, including electricity, food, and all bills, had funds that continued to be extracted regularly. That buys me time. It would likely be some time before it drained his accounts and everything stopped.

I settled into Mr Mann's old battered lazy chair and laid back and analyzed my situation. My vendetta has screwed up both Shane's and my lives, and I have to fix this. I let the tears come, sleep from exhaustion followed a short time later. I opened my eyes with some effort hours later; my eyes had swelled shut from the crying. Sluggishly, I made my way to the bathroom to splash water on my face. After raising my wet face from the sink, I took a look into the mirror, and matters were worse than I thought. Crying so much made my eyes swell, and that was bad enough, but that added to the cuts on my face from the tree limbs. To make my appearance worse, my swollen cheeks stood out from my face. I was barely recognizable as the woman from a week ago.

Standing there glaring at my appearance, I recalled both vicious blows from the Leather faced man. And shivered. I ached all over. That old couch was lumpy. The floor would have been more comfortable. I won't sleep there again. Between foster homes, I've slept in dumpsters that were more comfortable. I could have slapped myself if my face didn't already hurt. Why I just didn't go upstairs and get into his bed? Oh well, I thought I would remember that tomorrow, and now I'm sure there will be a tomorrow here. I need some rest and time to think. Retrieving Mr Mann's laptop, I learned the location of Ricky M's estate. This will be where I would begin my search for Shane. I pulled up the local traffic cams in my initial surveillance, and it was worse than I could have imagined. The cameras scanned the people patrolling the grounds armed to the teeth, and there was no sign of Shane.

There also were several women coming and going, many very pregnant. What kind of operation is that man running? Many of the women are trans-species of one sort or the other. I am trying very hard not to be prejudiced, but that was just weird. There were cats, dogs, rabbits, rats, and people with all kinds of long ears, long and short tails and I can't describe the shapes of eyes. He had something like that in mind for me, I'm sure. I do not know what was in the injection he put inside me. I have no intention of becoming part of his zoo, or kennel, or whatever. Did he get all of them pregnant? What the hell for? I know the country is struggling with population decline after drug O discouraged normal childbearing-age women from giving birth. But what he is doing is just too odd for me. What are the offspring? My thoughts have drifted.

Rummaging through the cabinets in the kitchen and finding some oatmeal put a smile on my face. Digging out a pot and adding water, I put it on the stove to boil. Searching through more cabinets, I located a bowl and spoon. Now I am in business. Minutes later, I added the oatmeal, stirred, then I was having a hot breakfast. While I stuffed my face, I waited for a solution to come. I have to think of a way inside that fortress of a home, but nothing comes to mind except surrender. Giving it a lot of thought, I have nothing left, no reason to fight or live. Shane is my everything. I got up and cleaned up my breakfast.

Walking through the house, I was still trying to come up with how to break into Ricky's home or business to find my husband. It's been a few days now, and I haven't come up with anything yet. My mind again drifted as I pictured Shane as a teen, then when we married, and finally, the crazed rage on his face the last time I saw him. Coercing Shane at such an early age, so I wouldn't be alone again was wrong of me. I had forgotten the extreme loneliness I felt before him. It won't be long before Ricky M's people search this place and get through my traps. After all, they have been one step ahead of me all this time. I won't be able to stay here for long.

Just months ago, I was safe and secure with my Shane. Now I'm living worse than a rat in a trap of my own making. At least if I knew Shane was dead, I would have closure, and if alive, I would have something to live for. I'm still not sure if I love him, but I am used to him. So, I have to know what his status is, therefore, surrender is the only answer. Fear gripped me at the thought of confronting Ricky M again, I languished in self-doubt at Mr. Mann's house for over a week.

Finally, a week later, I resigned to my fate. My emotions were a mixture of grief, rage, depression, then settling on rage again. Sitting here doing nothing was more than I could handle, I have no plan for getting my husband back. Finally, I could take it no more. I'm going in! I screamed to no one and everyone.

Using Mr Mann's financial account, I called for an Uber to drop me a couple of miles outside a house near Ricky's mansion. I doubt if my Shane is in there, but I have nothing else for a plan in mind. *I have always been a doer, not a planner, this will have to change without Shane in my life, I thought, but not today.* My brain is screaming, run, hide, fight, just do something. I just started walking after the Uber pulled off down the street before finding a place to stash my to-go bag. It's not likely I will remain unaltered long enough to retrieve my to-go bag. But just in case I needed it, I hid it under someone's porch so that I could retrieve it. It would have the account numbers and allow me to contact Mr Mann's accounts, as well as a Ride-share company for quick pick up if needed. Upon second thought, I think I will retrieve my small knife and, lock-picking tools.

After strapping them to my ankle with a leather strap, I was set to go into the Lion's den. Scanning around and for a moment, fear once again became my dominant emotion. I began thinking to walk away and start a new life. But I would probably just make another mess of things. My life is not worth much, but Shane deserves at least a chance, and picturing his face that was full of love and lust when we made love settled my nerves. Staring down the slope, I could see the house and the gated estate. I just stood for several minutes just a quarter mile away as I observed the set-up with the guards at the gate from my vantage point. The two of them sat in their little booth, chatting with each other as they waved people through.

The enormous building that loomed about a quarter mile from the gate shook my nerves again. Well, what the hell, I got nothing else and put one foot in front of the other? They will probably shoot me on-site, call the police, or have me arrested on trumped-up charges. None of this is new to me. Having no other plan or anything else to lose, I just walked up to the gate. As I approached on foot, confirming my initial assessment, I could see the large acreage of the place. There was no other way in. After scanning one last time, I could see that there were no vulnerabilities or weak points that my skills could use to infiltrate. Maybe a spark of genius will strike me on my way to the gate. My feet started moving, and my heart wouldn't let them stop. After gathering my resolve, I walked up in time to join a small crowd. Several heavily made-up women were walking through the gate, being waved by the guards. I expected the guards to say something like, "Hey, that's the woman we have been looking for!" The guns would all be at my head. I could see the canine features on the men's faces, making their features appear more menacing. The males at the gates had elongated faces and canines that peaked out of their thin lips. Both males had heavy brows and snout-like noses they were using to smell the women as they entered. Joining some heavily perfumed women that were walking in, the men barely acknowledged me. Now there was a constant stream of them.

The women paid no attention to me. Some were chattering with each other, while others were somber. Dressed in short skirts or skin-tight, almost painted-on pants and tops that left nothing to the imagination. None of these women appeared pregnant or over the age of thirty-five. I assume they were Ricky's next prospects for his drugs and mating rituals. I should have stood out in my ripped jeans and a regular-sized tee shirt. My hair was in twists hanging down, and I wasn't wearing implants or permanent makeup. That goes to show men really don't notice how much effort women put into their looks. I'd bet female guards would have noticed that I didn't look like the other women.

My whole entry was anti-climactic. We all walked up to the main building, which was much larger than I originally thought. We entered an elaborately furnished vestibule with large paintings (of people, probably family members) on ornately decorated picture frames. Huge tapestries and carpeted stairs completed the look. In my awe of the elaborate room, without thinking, I followed the women into a room decorated with Victorian Style furniture, screens displaying adults in many sexual acts, devices, and toys on every highly polished table in sight. Most of I did not know what to do with. Not only was I impressed with the furnishing, I was wondering why my entry was so easy. Yes, on some level, the orgy should have struck me, but damn, I lost my focus. Lost in my thoughts as I followed the curvy redhead wearing shorts so short they should have been thongs. Finding myself inside a room with sex toys on every surface shocked me into reality. All my self-sacrifice thoughts quickly turned into self-preservation. I can't do this.

"Oh no, wrong room," I said loud enough for everyone to hear as panic hit me. It was fight-or-flight time. I turned to leave when about four men joined us in the room, blocking the doorway we all entered through. Who the hell were we following to arrive here, trapped? I should have ducked out immediately or been paying attention. The men blocking my exit were all red-eyed like Shane was that night, minus the drooling and growling. My heart kicked up another notch. I started looking for another exit. The other women looked like they were dressed for a fun orgy, but not a rape session. Tension in the room rocketed up. My desperate scanning finally spotted the two other doors on the opposite side of the room. They were covered in tapestries and difficult to spot, and hopefully unlocked. I need a time out of sight to find a door to escape through. My frantic eyes landed on the door, the furthest away. While everyone was still getting organized, I was working on picking the lock. The women walked up to the men and performed a dance. I have little time now. I wish I could tell the women they don't need to work hard. When the screaming began, I almost had the door locked open.

The lock clicked open when I heard clothes tearing, and I was out. I ran out, leaving the door wide open, but didn't look back. At least I gave the women a fighting chance. Scanning the hall, I looked around and found another door and went into it. It was a broom closet of sorts. I looked for a weapon. No weapons, but there was bleach. I put it in a spray bottle. I thought I might need it to throw off my scent, so I sprayed the contents behind me as I moved through the halls. There was no one around when I opened the door.

The screaming had stopped; just a lot of grunting. I didn't want to know what was happening in there. I tried to get to the front of the house to get out, but there were too many people milling about, and now I was too scared to give myself up. Fear is a powerful motivator, but self-preservation trumps the fear. So I went back the other way through the house. I tried door after door, that were locked. I didn't jimmy the locks because I didn't know what was on the other side. The next door that opened to me looked like a servant stairway. Maybe I could hide down in the servants' quarters until the coast was clear. Then I could calm my nerves and blend in with the staff until I could escape. So I went in and went down the stairs to the bottom. I opened the door at the end of the stairs, and it wasn't to servant quarters. It was, to my disbelief, cells. Oh My God, a dungeon with people in them. It appeared to be about six cells cut into the basement, the cement floor and the walls. All lit with a weak light. If not for my enhanced sight, I would not have been able to avoid walking into walls. It was damp and musty and smelled like an old gym. No doubt there are rats, mice, snakes, and all matter of things down here. Turning back was not a good option yet.

Peering into the cells, I could at least see two moving individuals in separate cells. The cells contained a toilet only. There wasn't even a sink for washing. The men confined here were living worse than most domesticated animals. I was sympathetic, but I just needed to hide. None of this is my problem. I just kept moving. The men were in the same shape. They were unshaven, with all white beards and white hair and worn clothing. That was peculiar, I thought. I got near the first cell, and the man thing reached for me, grabbing my shirt. On instinct, I yanked my arm away as I sprayed him in the face with bleach. He said nothing, just backed away from the cage. Moments later, he put his nose in the air and smelled the air like a dog. I jumped away before he could lash out with his other hand. As he tore at my sleeve, he made an animal sound. What the hell? I peered at him closely. It wasn't Shane. Thank God, but this was worrying me. What kind of shape would Shane be in if he were here? I walked to the next cell, and it was empty. The next, another man similarly jumped at me, but this time I was on guard.

He sniffed me as well and said in a gruff voice, "Female, you smell good, come here."

Instead of spraying him, I felt pity for him and backed my way down to the next cells, but out of arm's reach. These men must have crossed Ricky M or something to warrant this treatment. Judging by the discarded paper plates at the corner of his cell, Ricky is still feeding them, so there is some use they provide him. The next few cells were empty as well. I turned to leave when I heard that familiar mulling sound. The cell I thought was empty wasn't, Shane balled up in the corner and was barely visible. Deep shadows enveloped him. If it weren't for my enhanced vision, the weak light in the dungeon would have kept me from spotting him.

Tears poured out of me, "Shane, Shane," I called out, "It's me, Jack. Can you talk to me?"

Out of him came a voice so deep and unlike his own, "Rachel, Kill Me. Burn this place to the ground." Then he fell back into the growling sounds.

I initially fell to my knees in anguish. Standing again, I put my hand through the bars. If he killed me, I deserved it. He looked at it, sniffed the air and with speed that took me by surprise, he rushed the bars of his cage. Snatching my arm and pulling me into the bars, he smelled and licked me. I offered no resistance while I looked directly at him. His distorted face surprised me, looking very animal-like. Shane's hair was white at the roots, and he sported an all white beard, but Shane was in there. His eyes still loved me. He gently kissed my hand through the bars. Then I fortified myself. Coming here to let him die here was not on the table. Looking him intensely in the eyes, I willed him to want to live. "I need help to release you. Will the others help me make Ricky M pay?" The others all stopped their movements simultaneously.

Like a symphony, they all growled out in unison, "Yes." Their unnatural voices made me tremble. Shane was here, and I could do this. Turning to look and face them, I asked, "How do I free you?"

One of them said there was a false panel over there. A hairy arm shot out of the cell, with torn clothing hanging down. He pointed with nails so black they more resembled claws. The rumbling voice echoed out, "Third from the top, just push it in, and it would pop open." Shaking myself out of shock and following his directions, I did so, and it revealed labeled cell numbers.

I looked at the cells and saw the small numbers above indicating the cells and pressed the buttons. The doors slid soundlessly back and the men were free. For a moment, I held my breath. They could all attack and kill me easily. I didn't think I even had any fight left in me if they did so. Shane ran to me, growling and wide-eyed. My first instinct was to run, but I changed my mind. Standing my ground, I will take whatever he gives, therefore, I stood in place.

He stopped in front of me and wrapped me up in his arms and said, "Rachel, I never thought I would hold you again. I have one confession to make before anything else happens today, and I don't care who knows this. I just can't take this to my grave like I planned. The day I arrived at Mrs. Miller's Foster home all those years ago, I had planned on my second suicide attempt. That was until I laid eyes on this tall brown-skinned, small-breasted but wide-mouthed, big-eyed girl I couldn't take my eyes off of. One look and I would follow her through the flames of Hell if she asked me to. You gave me then and still do a reason to live. Jack, I have never been enough for you, but I have always hoped that I could make you need me as much as I need you." He kissed me with so much passion my legs went weak. I was home in his arms again.

Then an unused voice interrupted, "Uh, I hate to interrupt, but you wouldn't be Rachel Lynn?" Both of us seemed to have forgotten we weren't the only ones in the room. The man, I use the term as loosely as possible, emerged out of his cell into the full light, as weak as it was. I instinctively jumped closer to Shane. He is the same man that grabbed for me when I entered the room. Observing my reaction, he looked down at my jacket and sniffed the air. He said, "Sorry about that. Your pheromones are so potent, and it is hard to remember who I really am. My name is Robin Miller. You know my Aunt Betty Miller. I am a freelance journalist. My aunt told me about Rachel Lynn, that goes by Jack." I was still perplexed. He read the look on my face and said, "She probably called me Steven." The light came on in my brain. "Oh yeah, the famous newscaster." He laughed, "Of course, that is what she would say. No matter what happens here, there is information that needs to get out. You need to make it out, and we will help you. None of us injected have more than a few months to live before organ failure. Ricky M's men have left us alive to milk us of our semen for profit on the black market. Ricky M's men deliberately gave us an overdose of some drug to kill us. The both of us, he showed himself and the other man, who was now out of the cage, have gained information that he doesn't want out. His men showed up and told us Ricky M needed us out of the picture. If any of us get out, we can pass the information on through the Post Office."

I asked, "The What? You must have been in here a very long time. There is no such thing as a Post Office anymore. He must have been in here way too long, I thought, because it has been about a decade since the collapse. Continuing, he said, I would love to burn this place to the ground, but there is no time now. We need to get what is happening here out. There is no chance of burning this place down. There are way too many fire suppression systems for that, but we can destroy as much as possible. We all know this is a suicide mission. We will die anyway, but at least we can take some bastards with us. Maybe we can free some others if the women are here. He stared at me intently. You make it out, find my aunt, and ask her to point you to the post office. Give them as much information as you can, but don't stay long with her. They will find you.

Once Steven finished speaking, Carl introduced himself. They both had wives when they were taken, and they didn't know what happened to them. They only asked for me to tell their wives they loved them and of their fate, but there was no time for details. Steven was the first to ease out of the door and waved that the coast was clear. We were all huddled in the hallway not far behind him. Since no one was looking for us, we agreed to try to walk as nonchalantly as possible if we heard someone. My heart was beating out of my chest. I was looking at Shane's back as he held my hand. The filth of their clothes and the horrible smell coming off the trio was almost more than I could bear. I don't see how this is going to work, but I can't think of anything else to do. We need out of this place. Shane insists on protecting me. Who knew he had it in him? I underestimated our roles for years, and he let me. We were hoping to find a door or a closet that held clothing so that we may blend in, but no such luck. I thought that would be way too lucky. Pointing out, I indicated the door I entered through, and we exited back up the stairway. Once we reached the top, we began to hear people talking and radio's clicking unintelligibly.

We waited until all seemed quiet and Steven walked out. He made it to the front door without an issue, then Carl followed out. Shane put one foot out and all Hell broke loose. The guards appeared from every corner of the room and in front of the two men. Shane shoved me back against the wall when he was hit with some kind of stun gun. I was touching him and was shocked as well, but I had the presence of mind to yank the leads out from his shirt before collapsing as well. It was enough to dull the shock that we received. My limbs tingled and were not accepting my brain's commands to move. My eyes moved to look at Shane, and he appeared to be suffering similarly.

A voice echoed through the halls. Ricky M was yelling out, "Jack, come out, come out wherever you are. I have your toys out here." Then I heard a loud Ugh, the sound of a punch in the gut. Ricky said in a sing-song voice, "I got all day to beat these pathetic men you brought into my home. Then I will find the last one you insult me with, and it will be worse for him."

Shane's head turned toward mine, obviously, he was regaining motor control. He whispered, "That guy is nuts," he looked toward a door across from us. Using two fingers walking, he indicated he wanted me to go into it. I tried again to command my limbs and found I could move, albeit clumsily. Waving my hands to him, I beckoned him to come with me, but I could see he was still struggling for more control and could not. I dragged myself to the door, getting more control with every step. The door was locked, but thankfully, it wasn't a complex lock. Unsheathing my picks, I lost precious seconds, fumbling around with getting my fingers to work. But after a short time, I unlocked the door. Then something flew out of the door so fast the door hit me in the face and I fell on my rear end. All I saw was a flash of white before everything went black. I don't think I was unconscious, just the wind knocked out of me. The drumming of feet running past me caught my ear, I looked up in time to see the naked rear end of women running past me toward Shane.

Shane flattened himself against the wall, trying to get out of the way of the frightened women. That we could tell for sure by the shape of her hips as one looked back, and we saw the swinging of her breast. The huge eyes on the young, pale face reflected sheer panic. The women had to have been trying that door at the same time I was picking the lock. Shane stiffly walked back to me, pulled me up and grabbed my hand, and we moved using the same path they took. I guess Shane hoped the chaos would allow our escape. He was right, naked women were screaming, many wrapped in the arms of men with lust in their eyes. The male guards were restraining the women as they tried to rape them, and the few females were trying to free the terrified young women. It was utter chaos as I watched. Several women were willingly in the throes of passion, a massive orgy in the residence, yet others escaping by running out the door to get onto the grounds. There seemed to be many more women streaming out that door than I thought possible. Leaving me perplexed, I don't know for sure what happened. I can only guess that some escaped women let the others free from wherever they were.

Ahead, I could see our two partners in crime-free and trying to steal a car by disabling the self-drive feature. They saw us and waved us to them. Carl was in the driver's seat when the engine gunned down. Steve was running to the passenger's side when shots rang out. A bright red bloom appeared right in the middle of Carl's forehead just as he touched the handle of the door. He fell straight back. We reached the car and dove in through the open windows while Steven hit the accelerator. We spun out of there. Looking back, the scene was horrifying, there were still women and men running around on the lawn, and now many of the men were naked as well. The whole scene was chaotic, but Ricky M was standing on his step, looking calm and staring directly at me. The Crazy Man was wearing an expression I couldn't quite read. Guessing, he looked like he was enjoying the challenge.

Steven shouted, "We have to find another car! Can either of you hotwire a car?"

Shane and I looked at each other, then at the same time replied, "Yes." I said, "It is better to look for late models. They have less chance of tracking devices or self-drive."

"Please head for Oregon Street! I shouted to Steven, turn down this street. I need a quick detour!" Both men turned to look at me like I had lost my mind. "Please humor me," I asked. Steven pulled over half a block away from where I stashed the bag with under the neighbors' porch. I ran to retrieve it and returned, then we were off again to find a good location. It is the oldest part of town, and it's only a few miles away.

As Steven drove, I asked, "What happened? How did you two get free?" He told me that when the women ran out, the smell of sex was so strong even he had a hard time resisting jumping them. He looked at me and I could see the shame, but I smiled, and he continued to speak.

"Every one of the guards dropped Carl and I, then grabbed women. Shane's eyes were roaming my face as he said, "I would have killed them if they touched you. However, I'm sorry I couldn't help the other women, but I had to protect you."

Steven spoke again, sounding a little weaker, "Me too, man. It is also important the truth gets out."

I was sitting in the back seat with Shane. Moments later, something caught my eye. I sat forward to get a better look at our partner in escape. That's when I saw the pool of blood on the seat and floor. I yelled, "Steven, you're hit! Pull over. Let me check your wounds!"

He calmly responded, "No, you will take the next car! I was shot before I ever ran. I am not long for this world, but you two have a chance. Get the story out." Shane and I looked at each other, and his eyes reflected the same concern mine did.

We pulled up to a lot with several cars. It looked like people probably carpooled from here. Shane and I got out and began looking for the type of vehicle we could use. Shane spotted it and got right to work. I walked back to Steven, who was just sitting in the car. His breathing was labored now, and I could see the blood seeping from the wound in his stomach in red streams. Steven saw me looking and chuckled, with blood also seeping from the side of his mouth.

With short, labored breaths, he said, "The man that caught me and locked me in the cage is the person that shot me. He assured it would take me a while to die. That's ok, I didn't expect to live through the day, anyway. The moment I saw you, I knew my time was over, but my hope was strong."

I opened the door and helped him stretch out his legs to make him comfortable. This is not a situation I handle well, I am not one that knows how to comfort people. I had a lot of questions, but even I could tell it wasn't appropriate. I needed to let this dying man get his last thoughts out. Shane rolled up in his newly acquired car, got out, and squatted beside the dying man. Shane had a towel in his hand and dabbed Steven's face, clearing the blood.

Steven's voice now was a whisper, as he had given up all pretense of strength. He whispered, "Go to my storage unit on Maypole Street, unit 468. Use voice code Sarah Stone. It is paid up through the end of the year. There is food and water to hide, but look for and play the cassette tapes, then get the information to my aunt."

Shane and I looked at each other for answers and asked at the same time, "What are cassette tapes?" Carl coughed up blood as he laughed. An antique recording device, never mind that you will figure them out. They can't be hacked or traced, and there is a lot of information on it. This is the real reason I have been killed. You don't have much time here, so one more thing, the unit next to it, 469 has a non-electronics car you can use, so ditch that one as soon as possible. Now leave, I want to die here alone and free. He had a violent coughing fit. A lot of blood came up, running out of his mouth and nose as well. I just stood there in utter horror. "Go", he said again. I got up and headed to the car. Shane lingered a little longer and whispered something to him. Then we turned to leave. We headed for the unit and found it within the hour. Everything was as he said. Once we got the other car, we ditched the stolen one in a grocery store parking lot. We locked ourselves in the unit; we were so exhausted. At a brief glance, the whole place looked like a museum relic from the 70s and 80s, and we found a futon and just rested for the night.

Chapter 6
Joy, Peace, and Heartbreak Year 2027

The next morning, I woke up in Shane's arms again. I felt safe and complete. I inhaled that familiar smell of my man filled my nose. Realization hit me, how I missed him so much. I got out of the small bed and started to really look around, trying to locate the food and bathroom. The unit itself didn't have a toilet. There were. However, disposable sanitary units emptying into a box that I could store for a few days until I could find a dumpster to get rid of it.

Next, I found soap and water wipes for cleansing, teeth, taken care of next, then hair. I felt pretty good and began looking for food. I noticed that almost nothing was electronic. The lights were battery or maybe solar, not sure. In any case, this place was set up for months of isolation. Finally, I found food packages again. They were the kind that heat when shaken hard. Good enough for me. I have definitely eaten worse.

A stirring sound pulled my attention from my finds to glance across the unit. I saw Shane was looking at me and smiling. I didn't bother to put my jeans back on. So, I was just wearing a bra and panties. I hadn't given it a second thought, but by the look on his face, he had. He got up, and before he could head straight for me, I pointed to the make shift bathroom.

He frowned, disappointed, but headed there. Once all that was bodily functions and cleaning was done, "So this is breakfast? It's better than dry oatmeal that I've eaten for the past weeks," he said.

"Oh, I'm so sorry. I know how much you hate oatmeal." I said with a pout.

Shane's eyes scanned my body and said, "Well, it was until my heroine came in to save me again." Like a man starving for me, he put his food down and pulled me to him and sprinkled me with kisses. Moments later, he slowed his pace and his hands roamed my body lovingly, mine did the same. It wasn't long before we were both naked and panting. We lay there entwined in each other. "Rachel, I want you to try to spare others, if only one person, the pain we went through in foster care. You need to find out where your eggs went and if your child or children are in loving homes." He said this while holding our hands up together, then kissing them.

"You and I can." He cut me off before I finished my sentence. "I won't be around, but a couple of months, you must make sure my death means something." His eyes held the truth and sincerity of his words. "We will go through this place and find all the information Steven gathered and make everyone pay legally. There is no need for a revenge rampage. Promise me."

Piercing me with his stare and prompting an audible response. "Right, Hi Jack? Those women were chosen to be raped by those men for a reason. Even if they consented, they didn't appear they knew what they were in for." I felt on edge. No revenge goes against my nature. I just didn't know if I could keep that promise, so I changed the subject. Blurting out, "The men, something was wrong with them, and they looked and acted like animals? What is the purpose of this Doctor Moreau's Island crap! Also, why did Steven purposely set this place up with no electricity? I would have to guess so that they couldn't track him. We know they track through smell, however, they still caught him."

I wanted to stay on my subject, but Shane held me with his eyes. "Jack, are we together on finding out these answers? Are we partners?" I rolled my body on top of him, filled with joy and some unidentifiable emotion. Letting my feelings reflect in my eyes, I said, "I love this partnership, and yes, I am in. Let's research and record the information and get it to Mrs. Miller, but first, I have a few other ideas." I said, laughing. I thought, *I haven't been this ever happy with my husband.*

My mind went over that fact Shane made every effort to protect me when we were at our home and Ricky's place. My heart burst with emotions for him, I always assumed I would be the one to protect what's mine, him. Despite being drugged to induce rejection, he only desired me more. Determined to make the most of his remaining months, I vowed to give him all of myself. Much later, we got around to searching through more of the boxes. I found a box full of white sheets of paper. I've never seen so much paper. In this digital age, it's just not necessary. Then I found an old-fashioned typewriter, or at least that is what *I think that thing was.* Shane found what must be cassette tapes and a machine.

Fortunately, the "cassette recorder" machine had instructions on how to use it on the back with extra batteries. The most shocking thing was the pictures Steven had in books. The first set of pics were of dead dogs, all breads, then it narrowed to pit bulls and Dobermans. We learned this is where all his research began.

These animals were descendants of animals Ricky M had cared for since his teen years and they were euthanized because they had COVID-19. Now, Ricky M's corporation is using synthetic animal DNA. Ricky M's company had been in existence for about ten years already at the time of the deaths. The thriving business's main clients were those who wished to add animal adaptations. Steven had collected boxes with tapes and photos of the necropsies. We both knew it would take a lot of work to compile this information. This is why he set this location up.

He must have known he needed a place off the grid where he could spend months compiling his research. He just didn't get here in time to finish it. I looked at Shane and smiled, "We will finish this for him. We need to find out for sure if women are being abused and expose him to the world." Shane pulled my face in for a kiss, "I love this side of you. Now we are past the petty revenge. I still want to find the child Penelope Matthews of Maryland gave birth to. That is our biological child. Maybe you can form a relationship with her birth mother and get to know our child." He picked up my hands and held them.

I looked into his eyes, and they expressed deep love. "I want you to be happy and open yourself up for our child. You can do this." Reluctantly, I couldn't ignore the sight before me: Shane's body was deteriorating, his skin taking on a darker hue, and his eyes displaying a noticeable yellow tint. I knew his organs were shutting down. However, they held an intensity that surprised and impressed me.

"Rachel, I was wrong. Going after Ricky M won't bring you anything but pain. Please leave the state after I'm gone and find happiness. Let me and all need for vindication go."

He never talked to me like this, like he was in control. He was dying, and he didn't want to hold anything back. I was barely able to hold the tears in, but years of not showing weakness prevailed.

The next three months were the best of all our years together. Open and honesty were how we interacted with each other. There were no distractions, and the chip I've always carried on my shoulder was gone. We were partners working on mutually desired goals. We spent the nights honestly talking about our childhoods, with the good and the bad. I laid my soul bare to the person I should have shared with all along. In the day, I learned to type on the antique machine and got good at it. Shane listened to the tapes, summed up the notes and dictated to me the conclusion.

The story was incredible. What I could grasp was that initially, Ricky M owned labs specializing in human reproductive health. Various people run these businesses he still owns. He developed the idea that humans needed to return to an earlier state in evolution in order to survive. He bought up small DNA companies and rolled them into his own. So what began as a quick money fad by some small companies he turned into more of a cultist following?

The premise was to amplify our natural human pheromones by utilizing animal pheromones. Because about 20% of men or women would not conceive children with their chosen mate, they had the wrong one. They needed the ability of the pheromones senses, like others in the animal kingdom, to enhance fertile pairings. He required the orgies and the DNA injections to trigger these urges. The fluid exchange between the sexes also provided the material for the DNA injections. Essentially, adding more animal and human hybrids was Ricky M's goal for the future of the human species. Now what Steven found was some women that claim rapes regularly occurred, but the police are in the pocket of Ricky M's organization.

Many women came to Ricky M with their significant other, and he deemed that person unfit. His people used drugs to find other viable partners to encourage pregnancy, whether you wanted it or not. There were details in the contracts these couples signed that allowed this. If you wanted to leave the area, or you left, no one could ever find you again.

Although no one will testify on camera, he also found that given enough of the DNA enhancements, other side effects occurred. The men would produce in the semen a hormone that, when combined with female hormones it, drives the men crazy with the need to have sex, so much so that they would rape. I knew that was what they used on Shane, and that is why they kept the men alive in those cells. They were overdosing them with this DNA enhancements. Shane and I discussed maybe ending our lovemaking.

Our concern was with all the drugs injected inside his body, if that would change my body chemistry as well. I don't care at all. Without Shane, it doesn't really matter to me what changes occur. I just need this time with him. Treatment at a hospital for Shane was out of the question. Ricky would find us easily, and he would separate us. We needed this time. I frequently wondered if Ricky

M had his Leather-faced man deliberately inject Shane with a more potent dose to hurt me or what purpose does he have?

Shane was growing more gaunt each day, no matter how much he ate or exercised. His hair turned white before falling out, and he no longer needed to shave his hair or trim his nails. I assume soon his organs would shut down soon. We were down to the last box of dictation when he could no longer walk. I had to help him with even simple tasks. He wanted to finish before he was gone. I took every day with him as the best day ever.

We laughed and hugged daily. He told me things about himself that he would never have before. He loved me more than life itself and would never have been about to continue without me. My body delighted in learning what it felt like to be loved. I always thought that I fooled him into thinking he loved me. It's hard for me to believe how wrong I was. My heart was racing with feeling for him. My sorrow expanded with so much feeling I would trade places with him if I could.

I don't know if that is love, but if it is, he taught me how. I will forever cherish the memories of him, and my heart will always overflow with gratitude for the countless years he stood by my side. He laid down one night and stopped breathing. I woke up to find he had typed out the last of the tapes himself. He must have sat down beside his work and passed. I chose a beautiful spot behind the unit, dug a hole and buried the love of my life if I could love. That still is a question in my mind. No words, no prayers, all those we have said.

It is now time for me to become the woman he and I believe I am. No one will stop me. I have a mission. I'm going to burn Ricky M's zoo to the ground or die trying, for I wouldn't be back here again. Functioning on numbly, I loaded up on what I thought was essential. The cassette tapes and notes I have plans for, so I brought that box with me and left it out for the last time. I drove the car left for us until I spotted what I was looking for, a suburban home in the middle of the afternoon with no one home.

I entered the home and walked through to see if it met my needs, and it did. There was no one home and an unlocked laptop, and it appeared to be a working family, so I had a little time. Ok, first things first. I put the box of cassette tapes and typed notes outside on the step. Then I ordered a courier to pick up the package at this address. I put to send the address of my high school in New York.

I included on the label "FOR YEAR 2029-2030," I figured this should have it stored on their musty shelves somewhere for a while until either I can recover it or someone can make use of the damning information. Now I'm going to need some supplies, but not here, so using a pin, I will have the drone drop them at the park across the street. I included a burger and fries since I have had nothing like that in months. So I have about an hour before my big supply package arrives.

I put everything back the way it was, closed the house up and went across the street. My food arrived a short time later. Sitting on a bench and eating my burger, I watched as a bike courier hefted the box of cassettes on the back of his electric bike. I started putting pieces together the information I learned from Steven's notes.

My packages parachuted down minutes after I heard the drone overhead. I loaded the box into the car without opening the boxes and drove off to my next stop. After a short amount of research, I got to the last residence of Carl, the man that was shot during our escape. I spent the rest of the day, night and most of the next day surveying the house.

The only person coming and going was a very pregnant woman, his wife. It took me only a few moments to confirm her identity on social media. The woman, however, had a very low profile, so I learned little about her personally other than her name Cindy and the general living situation. The woman was attractive, I would say.

Not a knock-out beauty, but cute. Her skin was pale, like the kind that doesn't tan easily. Her reddish brown hair was cut in a short bob, a short nose nearly flat on her face and a spray of freckles on that button nose and cheeks. She and Carl were married for seven years prior to his demise. After tracking down Carl's wife, I set up about a quarter mile away.

I learned that the woman worked from home while Carl was a private investigator. Pulling out and using my new binoculars, I looked for the drone platforms and mounted cameras that were as common in all homes as driveways. Nonetheless, they appeared to all be moved or missing from outdoor surveillance. Noting, the drone platforms were empty, and considering the debris on the platforms, it had been several seasons dormant. Whipping my tablet out of my bag, I ran a program that Shane, and I wrote to see what electronics the dwelling currently used. Oddly, there were a lot of internal cameras. Even in the bathrooms, pantry, and all closets. Once I gained control of the cameras, I quickly located Cindy.

The woman appeared to be doing her laundry. For a moment, I thought about how something so mundane as folding clothes was what I took for granted. Now what I would give to be home folding Shane's clothes. How annoyed I would get at his dropping his dirty laundry in front of the basket and the excuses he would give me. I found myself first laughing, then the prick of tears in my eyes. Anger rose up in my chest before I lost myself for a moment.

There are a few more pieces of the puzzle I want to get before I put a firm plan in place. Flipping over the information I had handwritten, I began to despair. Missing the little things we did together was so hard to get past. Shaking this off and stopping myself from going down that road, I need to get my head back in the game. Rising off my place on the ground, I ran away from the house hard for about a mile, then ran back. Breathless and heart racing, I was ready to allow my attention to return to the task at hand. I would have to work on putting the places I would likely traffic while in the home on a loop. I'd bet they moved the cameras from the outside to the inside. Sitting there, puzzling this out, why would she do that? The answer hit me, she was being watched, and they just used the equipment that was already located at the home. Ok, I began recording the view, and moments later, I infiltrated the home.

Cindy entered the front part of the house and moments later, she walked into the master bedroom to carry a laundry basket. I was there sitting on the bed, waiting for her. She gasps, then her face and shoulders dropped in resignation. Dropping her load on the floor in front of her, she said, "Ok, I've done everything you told me. I have nothing else to give. She said this while dropping beside me on the bed. If you are here to kill me or tell me you have killed Carl, then fine. You've beaten me. There is no more fight left for me. I will even accept the man chosen for me."

I smiled and put a reassuring hand on hers, saying, "Well, that's not what I want to hear. I want another woman to fight with me. Your husband and mine are dead, both killed by Ricky M and his dog pound. I don't know for sure why, but I will find out why and bring the place down. Are you in?"

She perked up, and a spark of hope shown in her eyes. Her lips went up in a smile for a few seconds, then dropped into a frown, "Shh, the cameras are everywhere." Her index finger went in a circle above her head, making the universal sign to encompass the house.

Confidently, I shook my head. "Not right now. I put them in a loop. We don't have long. I need to know what you do."

Shifting her legs and rear on the bed. Cindy got as comfortable as a pregnant woman could before speaking. "A family hired Carl to find their daughter, Ruby. They believed an animal cult took her in. You know, the kind that believes they were a specific species in some prior life and wants to relive that experience by changing species."

Rolling her eyes, then shifted positions on the bed again. "Well, a young woman named Ruby believed in her first life she was a rat and wanted to be with like-minded individuals. Anyway, she joined a group here and disappeared. The family wanted proof of life and whether she was here in this city voluntarily. Carl tracked her to Ricky's mansion. Ruby came out of the home and talked to him." She was now a cat with all the prosthetics. He had two recording devices, one that was the normal drone camera and one hidden one.

The drone camera got all the information he needed, and he transmitted it to the family. The hidden one was his nose ring, and then a creepy thing happened. He showed me what happened. It surprised him because he didn't remember most of it. Ruby got very close to him as though she was going to whisper in his ear, then sprayed him with something. Two ugly ass big men grabbed him and dragged him into a room. He woke. She was naked, and they had sex. He said he couldn't control himself.

Cindy stopped talking for a moment and looked at me as if she was imploring me to believe her. "I know it sounds crazy, but I know that man. That sex wasn't like him." I put my hand on hers and said, "I know. One cat did that to my Shane as well." She shook her head and continued. "My Carl told me this was going to be a blackmail attempt. We need to be strong. There is not much time, I'm sure, so that I will speed this up. Don't trust the doctors or police here. They are in on this. Many of the women involved signed some kind of agreement, so they benefit. Sex is the key. The catch is the partners aren't always the men you choose. Many of these women came here with their husbands, then Ricky M's doctors told them they couldn't be with him again. Carl wanted no part of that, and we weren't here for any of this. We were leaving, and these men broke in and took him. That was the last I saw of him. They assigned me a new man. I've tried to leave, but they are keeping track of me. There are others like me. The women send out something that when the men have sex with them, they become more animal-like. It is more than a cult. These people are being controlled through drugs and sex. They want children and control the schools and jobs. She rubbed her belly. You need to go. Some goons will show up soon and check on me. I will help you if given the opportunity."

I got up. "Can I get you anything?" She said, "No, thank you. Did my husband die well?" I said, "He freed me and others first. He gave me a reason to fight." She and I hugged, then I reached the door and heard a sniffle. I looked back and Cindy was crying while rubbing her belly. I purposely didn't ask about the pregnancy.

She spoke so low I almost didn't hear her. "There is one last important part." She sniffed up the snot, then grabbed a tissue from the dresser. Blew her nose and wiped her face quickly, then straightened her spine.

"They came for us one night. Ricky M's men dressed in all black and wearing leather masks. They shot Carl with a needle or something, then stripped me. Carl was out of his mind, with his bloodshot eyes spitting and growling. He looked at me as though he hated me. More malice than I think he possessed for anyone." She shuddered and sniffed.

Holding herself so she could get her words out. She spoke in a thick voice as the vile memories flooded her. "They said I was fertile now. After a few minutes, Carl went catatonic and just stared into space. Each of the men raped me, then one announced he was my husband now. The other men took Carl that night, and I never heard from him again."

She turned away from me and started crying. Retreating to her bedroom, then shut the bedroom door in my face. There were a few more questions on my mind, but I wouldn't get them from her now. So I left her alone in the house.

Chapter 7
I have allies?

I drove to Mr. Mann's home to sleep. Relieved, I found it to appear untouched. I curled up in his large bed, then planned out my next moves before falling off to sleep. After a not-so-comfortable sleep, my mission solidified in my mind. I have to visit Steven's Aunt, Mrs. Miller, then his wife. These people deserve the closure I will give them.

The next day, I was off to see Steven's aunt, Mrs. Miller. My head was full of information that I was still processing. Since I am no investigator and need someone to bounce the information off, I drove on. I hope this woman is the person to aid me. She was a college history professor in her early life. Then Alzheimer put her into a slow state of decline until this vape Drug X came on the market. Reinsertion into society is the niche that Shane and I filled. We helped these Senior citizens to reorient themselves with technology. It was a great business until I lost Shane. Recalling how scarce I've been the past few months, she may hate me for disappearing.

I just don't know, but I've got to try. Getting within five miles of the home, I parked the car in a lot, amongst others, so it didn't stand out. I packed a backpack with things I might need to watch her home, then infiltrate. Quickly putting on good hiking boots, a jacket, bottled water, and jerky, then I was off. I jogged for the first four miles, then walked while observing my surroundings for the last mile.

The mostly isolated home was on a one-acre lot surrounded by woods on two sides and an empty lot on the third side. The house sat about a quarter acre off the street in front of little lighting. I started looking for cameras and found a few, all aimed at her home instead of the surrounding area. As I looked out at the target house, I began plotting my infiltration. While using the device that Shane found attached to our cars, I mimicked the frequency signal they were using in the house.

Finding I was correct, I noted the home was bugged. Wow, why would anyone do that? There may not be a lot of cameras. I placed the ear mics in so that I could listen. Mrs. Miller, inside the home. I could see her through the windows, moving about and she sounded alone. While I observed her, I sat on the ground and made myself comfortable.

I no longer needed my binoculars, even in the low light. These changes in my body are amazing. I can almost see why some people would follow Ricky M's cult if they all experienced these enhancements. After a couple of hours, I cracked the few camera codes enough to put them on a loop, the same with the recording equipment. When the sun went down, I watched for another couple of hours and napped. When I woke up, it was completely dark. I got the kinks out and made my way to the house. I walked around to find the best softest point of entry and found it, then made my way inside. Once inside, I quietly checked the three bedrooms, kitchen, and small living room. Mrs. Miller actually walked past me twice without reacting to my presence. Finally, I returned to the master bedroom and made myself comfortable.

When she entered the room, I was sitting on the bed of the largest bedroom. I knew I startled her. She, however, said, "Oh, Mary Beth, you bad girl, you scared me. Why are you on my bed?" I knew right there she would help me. We both knew the cat wasn't a problem as she stroked the back of the animal in her arms.

I spoke loud enough to show I was sure of my work. "I disabled the bugs and put the cameras on a loop. It was long enough for me to come inside. I don't know when they would check on the bugs in your house." She put the cat on the floor, speaking while straightening herself. Me either, dear. Of course, I knew when that Sheriff brought that man with the leather mask on his face, it was to plant the devices and not to tell me about my nephew.

He introduced the man as another member of law enforcement. She chuckled at the absurd ruse. The Sheriff pretended he was informing me of the death of my nephew Steven. With a straight face, he told me you, your husband and my Steven were in a love triangle. This whole matter, regretfully, resulted in the death of the men and you on the run.

Mrs. Miller frowned as she spoke, "The sheriff wanted me to give him information on you. Don't worry, dear. I played the half-senile old woman. I didn't buy his story of his purpose for being in my home. I know you, Rachel Lynn. You would have eaten my boy alive."

She laughed out loud and so did I. She continued, "If he had as much as looked at you the wrong way. It is no way the three of you would have been in a love triangle." She laughed. "They had the wrong woman if they thought I was born yesterday. I played my part, though, so they would think they had an unwitting ally."

The older woman came into the room and sat down beside me and stared at me. "You look tired. You can go into the bedroom and rest. First, I want you to eat a decent meal, then get some rest. I have a feeling your life will get very challenging from here." I wanted to decline, but she was right, and I couldn't resist.

We ate a nice pasta and salad dinner over a light conversation. She talked about Steven and his need to land a big story, and he was researching Ricky M and the Matthews family. He firmly believed that the five Matthews brothers, along with a cousin who grew up alongside them, played a significant role in the decline of the US population due to their involvement with drugs.

They are so over-eager to repair the damage to decreasing the U.S. population from using the Drug Origen. The Matthews have taken such aggressive means to repair the problems as though they caused the problem.

As we walked, I realized she was leading me to a bedroom. Once we got there, she began preparing the bed. I felt so comfortable. Everything I came here to tell her just left my head as I saw the soft-looking bed with a fluffy comforter and plush-looking pillows. I undressed and changed into the long nightgown she laid out for me. It felt so good, like as if I had parents to take care of me. I didn't know how or want to resist. The camera loop should be fine unless someone was looking closely. I will just lay down for twenty minutes, then get up and talk to her. Fatigue hit me so hard that I fell asleep as soon as my head hit the pillow.

I woke up with the sun shining across my face, and for a moment, I thought I was back at home with Shane. Then I put that past me. Rose went to the bathroom and saw she had laid out a towel and toiletries. Taking advantage of the shower was irresistible, and it felt so good. Especially not knowing when I will do that again. Knowing that every moment I am here, I am putting this kind of woman in danger makes me feel guilty, but it feels so good to relax. I know my life from here on out will probably be on the streets. If I achieve what I have in mind, Ricky M will be out for blood.

She had breakfast ready when I came out of the bedroom. I said, "Wow, you are spoiling me, any chance you can adopt me?" She laughed and handed me a plate of fried eggs, bacon, and toast. I grabbed it and sat where a cup of water and juice sat. She knew I wasn't a coffee or tea drinker. Taking a sip of water, a fork of eggs and toast gave me a feeling of home. I finished eating so quickly that I barely tasted it.

I got up with my plate, rinsed it and put it in the dishwasher before Mrs. Miller was even half done. Her left eyebrow lifted and she said, "You eat fast." A warm smile graced her face and I couldn't help but return it. I didn't realize how much I really liked this woman.

Responding, I answered, "Thank you. It was delicious." Feeling the need to get down to business, I continued. My life while in foster care creates some habits that stay with you and eating quickly is one. I came to explain to you what I know of what has happened. To understand, I need help to put it together. I want to strike back, but I can't put things straight in my head."

She patiently chewed and swallowed before speaking, "Ok, dear, tell me everything." I told her from the beginning. Shane came home telling me a young woman blackmailed him out of my eggs. The doctor said my eggs weren't viable. Ricky M offering me a job with him, but I had to divorce Shane within the week.

He came that night and tried to make me choose to be with him. I refused. He drugged Shane with the intent that my husband would reject me. The drug backfired somehow and Shane became more animal-like. I wasn't sure if he would kill, rape, or both to me. He hunted me like an animal through the woods. It was terrifying.

Finally, I got away by outsmarting him, and they took Shane. I went to give myself up and, to my surprise, walked right into the mansion. The guards didn't apprehend me. They just let me walk in. I found Shane, Steven, and Carl locked up in a dungeon in the basement, and I freed them. We got caught during our escape.

Ricky M called me to come out. I ran and accidentally let the other confined women out. We got away in the confusement, but they shot Steven and Carl. Steven told us about his storage unit and his cassette tapes. The drugs shortened Shane's and others' lives of men that did things that Ricky M didn't like for only a few months. They even used their fluids to make new drugs to induce men to rape women so that they could use the crime for blackmail and pornography purposes. Shane and I transcribed Steven's voice, recorded paper research, and shipped it to my former high school in New York for hiding.

Steven was at first researching the source of the animal DNA Ricky M was using. Steven tried to interview some employees of the company. However, they refused. He secretly set up drones to record them and began noticing the behavior of the closest associates seemed unusual. He described them as automatons. Many with the most transformed appearances didn't speak and followed Ricky's orders only.

He suspected it was a cult. He learned of the parties, and the use of sex parties to reward participants, while not illegal, just frowned upon. However, he couldn't find rallies or speeches, things that most cultist use. He started believing these people may use drugs to alter normal behavior. Steven infiltrated the main house and gathered evidence. Next, Steven was making a plan to take his wife and leave. Taken at some point, shortly later, resulted in his death. He had several details on a crazy plan Ricky M and his family have to form plantations all over the country that they will rule over.

The weirdest part is he believed they had some drug that enabled all of them to live for hundreds of years. Looking at the woman, and I could barely look at her in her eyes. I don't know if your nephew was losing it at that point or this Ricky M really believes this. I lowered my head, shook it, and raised my eyes to her again. "What do you think?" The older woman said, let me give this some thought.

We both heard a vehicle pull up. She went to the window and looked out and said, "This is Ricky's people. Duck out the back!" I looked at her, surprised. "Are you crazy, woman, it's no way I will let you take these people on by yourself!" The men were out of the car at an unbelievable speed. One redheaded man came in the back door and the other in the front.

The black-haired man in the front reached the older woman first and grabbed her around her waist and covered her mouth. He sniffed her, then began dragging her back out the door. Before I had time to react, the other one had me in the same way. However, after he sniffed me, I could feel the bulge in his pants. Red hair removed his hand from my mouth and put it under my shirt and lifted my shirt while sliding his hands up to feel my breasts.

He put his face to my neck and smelled me again. He removed his hand from under my shirt and slammed my back against the wall. Removing my shirt and bra, in a quick movement, put his mouth on my breast. He fumbled with the button on my pants. I was so shocked I could only whimper. Black hair dropped Mrs. Miller and appeared by his side. He grabbed the first man by the back of the shirt to pull him off of me. Red hair fell on his ass, and with his junk still hanging out, I just stood there, unsure of what to do.

Mrs. Miller looked at me with wide-open eyes, in the same state. My would-be savior, without a word, grabbed me around the waist and began pulling me toward the door. He took a deep inhale, stopped, then unbuckled his pants and out sprung his erection. He turned me around so my back was to his front and pulled my pants down, entering me. Suddenly, black hair stopped penetrating and withdrew from me before hitting the floor.

I turned to see both of them rolling on the floor, fighting each other. Maybe Mrs. Miller and I should have made our escape, but sometimes instincts take over, and that happened. I screamed, "Stop! What the hell are you two idiots doing?" They both stopped, stood up, and were statue still. Their hands were at their sides and eyes forward as though they were waiting for orders.

I looked at Mrs. Miller, and she smiled widely like all the lightbulbs went off in her head. "Interesting. Now I got it. Tell them to go get in their car." I didn't understand, but what the hell, I thought before shouting, "Go get in your car!" They turned and walked back to their car and got in. How they managed to get to their car without tripping, I don't know. Now they just sat there, faces forward and pants unfastened and their penises out. I heard Mrs. Miller say, "Fascinating." She approached the passenger and asked the man, "Can you speak?" One Redhead turned to look at me.

I said, "Answer her." "Yes, of course." His voice was so rough and deep I didn't think it came out of him at first. I realized it was he just he didn't use it much. "Who is your boss?" She inquired. He looked and barely moved his lips, saying, "All the Beta's," I looked at Mrs. Miller and mouthed the word, "What, Beta's?" She turned back to the man and asked, "What is the name of your direct supervisor and who ordered you to monitor me?"

Still, without a lot of emotion, he answered. "Jillian and the Betas's of MDNA" She gave her next question some thought. I could almost see the wheels spinning in her head. I was so impressed at how she handled this situation I would not have made the questions so simple yet perfect.

She next asked, "Are the employees' spouses or significant others being watched with the same tech as I?" He answered, "Yes, they watch everyone."

Mrs. Miller asked, "Is there one Alpha the Beta's take their orders from, and what happens if they disobey?" The fixed glare of the men was on me. Although I wasn't the one asking the questions, that was a little unnerving. The answer surprised both of us. Redhead answered, "One Alpha, and we can't disobey."

Frowning, Mrs. Miller spoke to me, "I don't like the picture I'm getting of Ricky M's business. These people don't appear to have any freedom. It feels like a form of slavery. You need to shake that place up." Stunned, I asked, "You said what? Why me?" although I really knew the answer.

Ignoring my reaction, she said, "Ok, Rachel Lynn, here we have a chance to will improve the work lives of the employees. Teaching those Betas how to treat their subordinates would needle Ricky M. Do you think there any women held against their will?"

I couldn't think of anything else to do or say with her insanity and just kept my mouth shut as he responded to Mrs. Miller. He again answered in that flat tone, "No, all women are all well cared for." Mrs. Miller then asked, "When you leave here, is any harm going to come to me?" He said, "Not to my knowledge. We just wanted you to tell us why the listening device is not recording."

She said, "I have one more question. Why do you obey Rachel Lynn?" They both looked at the older woman as if they had never seen her before and, in unison, said, "Scent and voice, she is Alpha." They looked at me as though I dropped out of the sky wearing a golden crown. It surprised me they weren't on their knees bowing. Clearing my throat, I felt very uncomfortable. I will turn the listening device back on.

You can return and tell whomever you report to that all is well here. Without a word, they started the car and drove off. I turned to Mrs. Miller, pleading with her, "What the hell, please help me with all of this?" "I think I know what has happened here," she smiled as she walked out, further away from the house. "First, go turn the bugs in the house on and then join me out here."

I did so and brought out a pair of chairs. She asked, "A few years back, did you catch COVID-19? Was it a severe case?" Well, I didn't see that coming, but now I'm game, so I simply answered. "Yes, on both counts." "Ok," she said, "This is what I surmise from what you told me, what Steven said to me on his research, from the media and my observations of the history of this area. Ricky M, his four brothers and a cousin, Clifford, are now infamous as wealthy corporate business owners.

They proclaimed they were helping the country to recover from the largest population decline in history. Ricky M owns the company ANIMAX as well as several others. Steven was researching how

Ricky M got started with the idea of pack and herd animal's reproduction. This developed into the synthetic DNA that is all the rage with young people today. Well, what most people don't know is that he had a severe case of COVID-19 and altered vocal cords.

He still has long COVID. Ricky M is a brilliant man, holding various Doctorates. Becoming confident of foreign DNA was the answer for the man. Ricky M injected himself with canine DNA to repair the damage. As a result, his voice became more baritone than it is now. Steven believed that some of the greatest leaders in history had specific chords in their voices that made people want to listen to them.

This led to Steven's interest in Ricky's company after learning of Ricky's unnatural influence over people. I'm guessing Ricky M used this in combination with his DNA splicing to enhance this to create his followers. He is constantly bringing women in for sex parties, so I would guess he needs to reinforce the DNA cocktail with female hormones. This would explain why their distraction when the women ran through the room during your escape.

The men here also couldn't control themselves around you. "Yeah, but they were raping me at first before I spoke up," I said.

The woman chuckled, "They were. You know, men sometimes confuse all urges with sex. Your voice must have those same alterations as Ricky M's, making them obey you. Whatever he injected you with probably boosted your natural gifts. Because you already have the female hormones, you don't need the supplemental injections. He likely learned this about you through doctor's visits or was looking for candidates like you. This is probably why he tried to hire you initially so that he could use you. You can be a direct challenge to his hold over his followers. Now it would be better for him if he had killed you because together, we can make his life Hell."

She smiled wickedly and so did I. "Now I believe you can control all of his men. However, as for his women, I am not sure what is the level of their loyalty. Aside from the women, he has been running the scam to steal the eggs from unsuspecting couples and using them to blackmail the men. I have a theory for the reason as well. I believe he is selling at a low cost these eggs, having them fertilized between himself and others of his choosing. This way, these children can will be under his influence when he comes for them." I interrupted, "Therefore, mine and Shane's genetic material went to Maryland for Penelope Matthews so that he can have a spy in his cousin's camp?"

She gasped as her eyes lit up, "You said, Penelope, that's his aunt and Clifford's mother. Oh, he is a real bastard. He is planning on controlling his own cousin. Well, they are people I understand and travel in the same circles with. I will go there and talk to her, as well as go to New York and look through Steven's notes. Meanwhile, you need to disrupt Ricky M's life as much as possible." She smiled.

We both know what you are capable of. Keep him off balance until I can gather something substantial on him. Remember, the smell is everything. If you still menstruate, that blood is the most potent. You need to use every tool at your disposal. Other than that, get close to the women involved and find out if they are inside this cult by choice. If not, show them how they can use their 'assets' to improve their situation.

We set up a time and method of regular contact. She showed me how to use this antiquated machine that is so obsolete tracking it is unlikely. I thought as I watched her use the fax machine. This must be where Steven got the idea of going old school to avoid high-tech surveillance detection. We walked back inside, and I packed up my belongings. She added some non-perishables. I jogged the miles back to my car, and I took off to survey the home of Ricky.

I found myself in a nice wooded place about a mile away to scout the corporate building of Ricky's DNA business. I just settled for calling it the pound. The people coming out of that place were unbelievable, there was definitely a canine theme going on there.

There were so many two-legged canines coming in and out of that place. Undoubtedly, the people coming and going in and out of the place resembled a pound. Pulling out my retro Polaroid camera out of my backpack, I started snapping.

My first picture was of a guard I named Beagle 1. He had a flat, long body with sandy brown hair. He had either grown or augmented floppy brown ears, reminding me of a beagle. So I scribbled that as his name on the back of the picture and the time of day. Stepping into my camera range, next was the man I affectionately dubbed "Big Doberman".

Now, this guy was a piece of work. He had an elongated nose, dark skin, and he was huge, probably 6'6 or something. Best of all, the long pointed ears with ear-studs all along his outside the ears. The two of them were on guard duty for about six hours while I was there. It appeared most of the visitors I saw to be vendors, with a sprinkle of female visitors. There was my old buddy Sandy from 2 pm till 4 pm. Dressed in a blue pinstriped skirt suit, expensive pumps and bag, her hair was up in an elegant chignon.

Then there was a well-dressed man I would peg as a lawyer who visited between 330pm and 430pm. Later, I would check Social Media for his face if he pans out to be significant. Waiting for a change of shift, I broke out my kale chips to snack on. It finally came around 8 pm. One look at the guys, and I named the replacements as Pitbull and Greyhound. It was time to pack up my gear and after another hour. Finding myself a hotel to check into, I booked online with Mr. Mann's credit card. I am pretty confident no one is looking for me, at least not yet.

Desiring a restful night's sleep, I am cautious and have taken the prudent step of setting up some traps before finally settling in. The next morning, I began laying the groundwork for the plan that I was planning. I looked through social media and found some generic memos the company MDNA has sent out to a huge mailing list.

After I copied the letterhead, I plagiarized a similar letter the Human Resources Department of the company MDNA sent out by altering a few words. Adjusting it to inform the people on the mailing list, the company may send out a representative to conduct wellness checks on some employee spouses.

The representative will use a quick survey, only ten minutes of time. I figure this would give me enough time to get an idea of the home. Of course, I will stake them out an hour before and after. The next thing is to find what vendors I can access and interrupt deliveries of. I am sure my hacking skills but they aren't good enough to get into any of MDNAs Corporate information, but with some smaller vendors, I can be a nuisance. Last, I need to set up a six-month residence for myself. It won't be long until I am discovered. After all, my coup de gras is to test my power over Ricky M himself, and I may need a place to run if I fail.

Chapter 8
Phase I plan

My plans took about three months of detailed surveillance, and I've come up with a three-phase plan. Today I will implement Phase I of my plan. I know my Shane wanted me to walk away and leave this alone, but I can't. My confidence is back, and now I have an edge with the voice-control. I will have my vengeance.

I narrowed down the six women I wanted to visit. After I sent out a reminder memo, I went off on my visits armed with phony credentials. The first was Doberman's wife. The two elementary school-age children had gone to school and mom worked from home. I found all the employees lived within a twenty-mile radius of each other. I don't know if this is common or not, but convenient. It was a modest rambler in a well-maintained neighborhood.

The grass was trimmed, and there were no toys or bikes in the yard and trim bushes. Using some of my clothes from my stunt with Sandy, I felt confident in this phase of the plan. I had a black wig with the hair in a bun, thick black glasses and a neat black skirt suit. Parking in front of the house, I strolled up the walkway, then I put my face in the door camera. Using my most pleasant voice, I said, "My name is Ms. Pulley, and I am here from the company to do a quick survey. Do you have a few minutes?"

A moment later, I got the AI reply, "Yes, come in," and I heard the doors unlock. I walked into a modest living room with an open floor plan so the kitchen and living room were easily visible. I stood and waited. Out came a slender woman with dark brown skin, about 5' 7 and a wide-mouthed smile. She spoke in a high-pitched but pleasant voice. "My name is Thelma Myers. I hope this is a brief visit." Trying to speak as much confidence as I could, "Yes, just a few minutes of your time, and I'm Ms. Pulley." I looked at my tablet and asked, "What is your favorite food?"

She looked quizzical but answered. "Strawberry Crêpes with whipped cream," she replied with a smile as if remembering the taste. I looked at my tablet and asked, "Where is your favorite vacation place?" She was getting this. It was about her and she answered, "I love cruises to The Caribbean." Now I've got her a little more relaxed. I threw in a question with the two of them. "If you and your husband attend movies, what genre do both of you favor?" Her face never changed. She answered, "We love comedy. We saw one last week." Just one more question. Your previous husband, I said with a reassuring smile, "The one before you lived here and worked at the company. Would he have taken you to the movies on a weeknight?"

Her eyes grew suspicious, but she answered without hesitation, laughed a little and said, "Oh no. However, my current husband really likes his position, and it's really a close-knit community here. We all look out for each other, and our life is more secure." Ok, I said, "Please give me your key fob?" I held out my hand in expectation. Drawing her eyebrows together and scrunching up her face, she said, "What, why, no!" I only asked to see if she was under my control. Relieved, I could clearly see she wasn't.

After what I did to Shane, I no longer feel comfortable with the need to control others unless absolutely necessary. Not giving her a hint of what I was thinking, I covered. Putting on a disappointed face, I said, "I just want to make sure there is no code stamp on the back showing it is one of our corporate models." She held it out of my reach to show me. I thanked her for her time and asked, on my way out the door, as she had spoken to her first husband lately. Her smile dropped from her face. Her eyes showed a long sadness.

A moment later, she recovered and plastered her smile again. "I know you really aren't from the company, but I will answer your question. Since the divorce, I have not heard from my ex. I assume he is well. Is there anything else I have work to do?" I was a little surprised and waited to see what she would do. "Are you checking on my well-being? She rubbed her belly more protectively than anything." I got what I needed and thanked her. "How did you know? I wasn't from the company?" I asked. She had such an old soul in her eyes, smiling, "You don't sound like a robot."

Thelma thrust out her hand as she snickered to herself. Initially, it seemed like she wanted to shake my hand, but upon second thought, she decided against it and opted to affectionately rub her belly instead. "Give me a way to contact you and I will inform you if there is a problem. I didn't choose to conceive this child, but it is not so bad, and I am well cared for. Although, if there were something I would like to see changed, it is how the Betas at the company treat their subordinates.

They get all the best perks while just sitting in their ivory towers, raining decisions on the workers like my husband. You are the one that will give the betas at the company a hard time, won't you?" She laughed, "Never mind, I got my answer, do what you do. My eyes roamed her face before responding, "I will tell you what. I will think about it." Her face grew thoughtful, and she said, "You need to contact me again. You are welcome. I won't turn you in. That woman, I thought, is very perceptive. With that, I got in my car and drove to my next woman on my list.

All the questions, except the last two, were irrelevant. The last three were to see if the company improved her marriage if she had to follow my orders, and if she had feelings for the ex-husband. They probably forced her to divorce. I did the same to the next few women and got similar responses. In conclusion, at least the wives seem satisfied with their current situation. Their answers were relaxed and genuine. The husbands spent time with them. They still had hopes and dreams, although these men weren't their original choice. So all is well there, so it is time to move on to Phase II.

Now the fun begins, with the blessing of both Mrs. Miller and Myers. Really wishing I was a fly on the wall so that I could see instantly the results. I did somewhat set up a potential spy, however, I'm not sure of her ability or full cooperation. I sent over a congratulatory present for the birth of Cindy, Steven's wife's baby, with contact information and a covert means to contact me. On her trash day on Tuesday, out of the dirty diapers in a blue bag, she will give me a recorded chip of gossip about the area she wished for me to know. After all, how many spies would search through the dirty diapers trash? I just wanted to know what the other women thought about the company or the changes I had planned. I would simply have to wait to see if that panned out.

With that part of Phase I complete, I moved on to the more important part of the mission. I need to test the soft points of Ricky M's Animax corporate office, where most of the people work. My first bit of fun was simple. There are air vents that circulate cinnamon-scented air for the normal workspaces. However, when there is a party, they switch out the canisters to a mild form of marijuana, a common practice nowadays. Almost every event planner has incorporated the drug into their offerings since it became federally legal years ago. I arranged for the distribution company to switch the normal cinnamon for the marijuana now on an average workday. The company doesn't know when or how long the parties last, so they never questioned the request.

I had it pumping marijuana for the past week. Next, I changed the employee break room. It has several fountains to retrieve sparkling water. They drop to fill cups while you watch, then seal so that they can be easily carried by people. This is common, however, the betas have sparkling wine water. They are a little high all the time. Well, I changed this to the employees with the wine and the betas with sugar sparkling water. The betas probably didn't notice. I'm sure they are high on far more than alcohol, anyway. I was laughing to myself the whole time.

For the next six months, I "Hi Jacked," everything I could think of. Here is a list of my best performances; there were, of course, numerous failures. I'll try not to think about those. Here they go: I had the vendor put a bubble maker in the sprinkler system, then triggered it about a week later; I got control of the lighting system in the employee warehouse and had the lights flash while I played "Hokey Pokey; I did that many times. The betas lunches and employee lunches were switched at various times. I had the betas sent McDonald's burgers randomly. During shift changes, I had the music blast at full, the classic song, 'Who let the dogs out.' I have been getting weekly updates from Cindy. She told me at first, the employees were a little scared at how the betas were handling the pranks.

They worried they would take it out on them. The annoyed betas gave up the search for the culprit after a couple of weeks. They confirmed it was probably an outside source. Cindy asked me, and how did I get the dye in the water of all the bidets? I wondered why, of all the things I did, that was the real puzzle to her. After explaining how it was done, she explained it was now a matter of a running joke. A few of the betas came out with their faces stained with red dye. I laughed so hard I cried. I honestly couldn't explain how or why one would put their face into a bidet.

Other than that, I heard the productivity has improved and there has been almost no one sick. It is like the employees go to work in a great mood, waiting to see what happens next. The betas have made impressive strives to improve the relationships with their subordinates, with the hopes the pranks would stop. Confessing to her, I told her I was running out of ideas. If she would like to take up the fun, we could meet, and I could show her how. She sent me a message back and had other women that wanted to do it as well. I certainly didn't see that coming and had to give it some thought.

I agreed to meet the women and get a better picture of what they wanted. We met at one of the local parks at noon the following week. I arrived around 1100, parked about two miles away, and scouted the area. It was clean. There was no one there at the time. First, jogging around the playground, I examined every suspicious bag, cup or leaf, looking for listening devices. I must admit I am no expert, so I could only do the best I could. Once satisfied, I found a tree-lined area with heavy brush. I waited until 1210 to approach the women once they were seated at a bench.

There were four small children nearby playing in the sand that the three pair of eyes were focused on. I spotted Cindy immediately. Her petite frame was wearing a long flowery dress. She had a baby harness affixed to her and was bouncing a baby while looking for me. The other two women stood with her. They were both facing the opposite direction of where I approached. One was tall, probably a little taller than I. A heavy wide hipped dark-skinned black woman with her hair pulled up into braids pinned into a ponytail.

The other woman was a little shorter than me but still taller than Cindy. The second woman was medium brown-skinned with an average build and hair braided up into a top bun. When Cindy saw me, they both read her face and turned to face me. They wore welcoming smiles and were both thirty-something. I relaxed and approached. I said, "Hello, Cindy, then I introduced myself."

Knowing I had never given Cindy my real name, but I felt I could give out my first name safely now. "My name is Rachel, but most people call me Jack, nice to meet you both," I said while extending my hand. The larger woman took my hand in a firm grip and said, "I'm Amy. Nice to meet you, Honey." She spoke with that southern drawl that showed somewhere like Louisiana, Georgia, or Alabama. Next was, "I'm Stacy." she had the same accent as I've heard common from here. I said, "Just in case cameras are recording, let us refer to each other by our favorite food names.

For example, Cindy is Strawberry Crêpes. I am Tortellini." Everybody laughed, including myself. Amy likes this and got into it. She spoke with that drawl of hers, ok, "I am a chocolate beignet." Then Stacy thought carefully, and her eyes lit up, "You guys are making me hungry, so I'm going to say my favorite food is anything teriyaki." Cindy spoke up, "Let's sit. We don't have a lot of time, although this was fun. Life here isn't awful for any of us, but you've made things better.

We want the chance to hold the betas in check to keep up their treatment in case they slip. All we want is how to make this happen. You don't have to give us anything, just the blueprint on how we can find it for ourselves." I have to admit. I couldn't help but show my surprise. I thought they were going to ask to know everything about me personally. If they did, I would have walked away because I could go to jail. I smiled, "Ok, then just observe the comings and goings of the vendors.

Then find someone with some hacking skills. They don't have to break into anything that is highly protected. Just files that have minimum security. Then get creative. Some things won't work. Many of my schemes didn't work. I poured the popcorn into the heating vents and hoped it would spray popcorn on everyone. It didn't. They had some kind of animal trap that caught and disposed of the seeds. Things like that happened. Just use perseverance. Most files I couldn't get into, although I had great ideas for them."

The three of them smiled and stood. For a moment, my heart jumped and I thought I had said something that incriminated myself enough for them to turn me in. I was going to jail. They looked at each other and laughed. Crêpes, still laughing, barely got out. "We have got some ideas. This is going to be fun. Thank you so much." Beignets said I own the dress shop AZ's downtown. Just like most shops, most deliveries are by drone. I'll give you my drone code if you need to get messages out or in anywhere using this drone.

Just order this dress, it is out of stock, but I will recognize it. I will send a confirmation. When you get it, send your request." Wow, this is a real boon for me, a way to get or receive messages and friends other than Mrs. Miller. "Thank you," I said sincerely. Within the next few months, I will confront Ricky M with his crimes, chiefly being holding the men prisoner and then milking them of semen. Second, manufacturing that rape spray used to blackmail men. Last, as with the women.

The forced divorce and arranged marriages in the name of fertility. Since the women I spoke to seem well-cared for by their new spouses, I don't want to expose them. Because I just want him to make sure he knows if he cannot treat the employees well, I will expose him. I need to know if there are any women being held against their will. As hard as I've tried, I could not find out. I will contact you monthly. I gave them Mrs. Miller's contact information. If I am out of contact with you anytime, please contact her. Maybe she will call out the cavalry, or at least she will know my fate. Good luck with your endeavors.

Strawberry Crêpes spoke up suddenly with, "Wait." I got the impression that she had been building up the nerve to ask me. Her face got very serious, "Look, when my husband and I first made the decision to come here, we brought a couple with us. They were female partners who wanted to each have a baby. They went into the Animax building for a consultation and I have never seen them again. I have only received short clipped texts from one of the women stating she is pregnant and will remain at the complex until delivery. Please, if you go into the place, check out the pregnancy ward to check on the wellness of the women." She gave me her friend's name, I couldn't promise I would find them, but I could at least check out the maternity ward if I got into the building. We all got up and split in separate directions. I was feeling more confident than ever. I had a mission and nothing was going to stop me.

Chapter 9
Year 2029 Phase II

I got back to my current temporary home, a camper that Mrs. Miller had her cousin rent for me. After checking my messages left for me on a fax machine to see if anything from Mrs. Miller had come in, and still nothing. It's unbelievable she was able to not only rent this camper that looks like something straight out of the twentieth century. The added bonus is it one that still has an active landline.

It crossed my mind maybe Ms. Miller is more than what she appears. However, I trust her, so I just went with everything and I won't question her. I am eagerly anticipating the progress of her investigation before proceeding to Phase II of my plan. She is going to meet with some people as well as thoroughly read Steven's notes. Her academic background is essential for providing weapons I need to use against Ricky M.

Let's face it, I said out to no one. I need more than my voice to overpower him. Some real hard-core evidence that can I'll take to a court of law if I have to is what I'm hoping for from Mrs. Miller. My anxiety level was leveling up, and I needed to burn off some energy. I put on some sweats, running shoes, a hoodie, and a scarf and wrapped my face. Ok, I thought taking a long run should help me to think, so I bolted out the door. As my feet pounded the road, I thought of what I wanted to accomplish. Yes, I mused, I want Ricky M to see my power over his men and to confirm if it is his agenda is to use his power over men and rule his own kingdom.

The reason for the pranks was to gauge the extent of his influence and soften him up and to improve my friend's husband's work life. I wanted to annoy him and his people enough that they knew their business still requires them to respect their subordinates. Not this weird voice control that Ricky M exercises over them, especially women, as though he is some kind of God. After all, I have the same voice enhancement, and I'm not going around ordering people to obey me.

My dream is to see myself marching right in there, past his guards and into his office. Wearing my power suit, standing over him while he looks at me in awe. Yes, smiling at the scene in my head. I am going to tell him I know that he and his fellow schemers like Sandy are using drugs his company produces. Then blackmailing innocent men into selling their wives' eggs. He held my husband, dosed him with a DNA drug that made him crazy.

After capturing and imprisoning him, he milked him of the hormones produced in his blood against his will. I have the proof from the journalist, Steven. At least, I hope Mrs. Miller will come up with concrete proof. If Ricky M doesn't retrieve my property and stops this disgusting business of forced marriages, I will turn him to the Feds. If he tries to harm me, I will have his own guards hurt him. I laid back on the old couch and smiled, just picturing the outcome. However, I know I have a lot to bank on, so I need Mrs. Miller to have the proof and clarify a few missing pieces. Like, why is he forcing marriages at all? Is he profiting from the theft of both male and female reproductive material? I understand the birth rates in the country have declined sharply since the vape drug O came on the market. Why do Ricky M and the other Matthews care?

This is a risky venture for me. After all, he still could kill me before I can get help, but it is a risk I will take. After all, I promised Shane I would burn his house down, and I am doing it the best way I know how. I wrote out everything I am planning with the idea that once I hear from Mrs. Miller and she confirms she has proof, then I will begin the last phase. However, if I don't return within twenty-four hours, the information will go to the media. There is no guarantee they will print, but that is all I have.

Over the next few weeks, I did more contingency planning, but I was getting bored. I continued to communicate through messages with the women: Strawberry Crêpes, Beginets and Teriyaki. I found the use of the dress shop to pass messages was great. They kept me informed of the gossip they had learned. It really wasn't anything I could use, but it was nice to have someone to talk to, even through messages. They also were aware of my plan to confront Ricky and said if I don't report back in a timely manner, they would try to get a message to me. In my boredom, I thought about staking out Sandy's place again, but that woman scares me. I don't think I can handle her.

So, Jessie, it is. Where is she, I thought? She has become better at covering up her Social Media profile. I started searching through popular college sites with no luck. I searched for sports like football, basketball, etc. Still no cigar. I was losing hope when on a fluke, I checked out dog-walking sites. Jackpot, not only was she there, there were invites to parties hosted by the MDNA company. I followed her down the links and found the invitees had to sign a legal document stating that they were okay with participating in sex acts while at the party. The women agreed not to sue the company or other participants if anything distasteful happens.

Because they are willing participants. I thought, well, that explains how Ricky M keeps his orgies quiet, with the Non-Disclosure contracts the guests sign. The parties give those taking part guests presents like chance books to win particular surgeries, enhancements and legal DNA drugs. *These kids taking part are crazy,* I thought. I got just enough information to have a good place to locate Jessie, so I could harass her once again when a strange whirling sound started. I stopped dead and started searching the place for that sound. What the hell was it? Finally, I found the source. It was that damn thing Mrs. Miller said she would use to contact me, and it was sucking on paper on one end, then spitting it onto the floor. I picked up the paper, and it was a letter to me from Mrs. Miller. It read as follows:

I have successfully found and read through Steven's work. I would sum up what you currently need to know. Ricky's DNA research began because he found his voice had changed after experiencing Long Covid. He could use this change to make its power of suggestion susceptible to many people. There are reports of other women claiming the INVITRO division of his company seem to have lost their genetic material more often than any other company of its kind. This is a powerful indicator that there is something illegal, but I don't have proof. They compensated each of the complainants. I think he is using their eggs to spread his own genetic material. The purpose of, which I surmise, is to make sure he has devoted followers for the next generation. I possess a detailed list of recipients who have received his product, and it is highly specific.

Including his aunt and a couple of brothers. I have tracked down his Aunt Penelope and her son, Clifford. They would like to speak to you. What I have for sure is the couples that come to Ricky's MDNA or other companies have an excessive rate of divorce. Then they are married to other members or new people brought in. He is making his own matches, and I think he is doing this using force, whether drugs or his voice. If you insist on confronting him, I believe your voice will be stronger because he needs the female hormones. I hope you will reconsider this approach and wait for more information. When you conclude your business, send me another fax as I showed you, and we can set up a time to talk. I have sent a man named Ralph King from this area that I have worked with in the past. He has interests in the Matthews family and will like to assist you. He said he would find you shortly and help in anyway he can. I expect to see you within the month. Don't forget to burn this document like we discussed.

Mrs. Betty Miller

Well, there are a few new things, but other than that, I think I can do this. I envision myself strolling in, telling Ricky M I know about the girls, his matchmaking and sex parties. They will stop now. I will tell him. He will think he could use his voice over me or call for help. My presentation of evidence on a file would play on his screens. Oh, how surprised he will be when he realizes he is no longer the one in control. His world would crumble before his eyes. I smiled to myself at how he would grovel. I would remind him how he killed my husband and two other men and deserved to pay. Then I would stroll out of there and all the employees would drop what they were doing and follow me. He would sit there with nothing. Yes, it would be magnificent. That day I would dress in my best power suit and heels, pin my hair in a bun and apply my makeup like a professional. I'm going to burn his world down.

Once I finished daydreaming, a thought sprung to mind. Although I don't yet have a smoking gun of information, I could do some prep work. Thinking about this, I thought, I don't know the location of Ricky M's office or where pregnant women go for treatment so I could check on them. I doubt if he chances, letting them go where he wasn't in control. Next, what is the level of my influence on more highly trained guards? Needing some information on the inside of the business, I planned an infiltration. Crêpes told me of a part-time house cleaning job I could use there. An acquaintance of ours, Thelma Myers, who I met while conducting surveys, got a job there recently. We look enough alike I could pass for her. The plan was to hide in her car as we entered the gate. We would dress alike and get in. The guards didn't look too closely. She could go inside when there was one guard on duty. As soon as that guard goes on their rounds, I would walk in dressed like her to fool the other guard.

The next day, I implemented Phase II of my plan. Seeing Thelma Myers again was a pleasant surprise, and she was all too happy with sneaking me in. She snickered as she explained this was similar to one of her favorite video games. The first part of the plan worked flawlessly, and I was inside on the first floor. My supplies included some lock-picking tools, a pregnant belly costume, and saved menstrual blood. The last part was grouse and disturbing. However, Mrs. Miller once told me my influence would likely be stronger with it. Hopefully, I wouldn't have to talk, but I couldn't take the chance. Some people would be more resistant to my voice.

With my thanks, Thelma and I celebrated with high-fives, and she strolled off in the other direction. My goal is to find where Ricky's office and to discover if the pregnant women were being held here. Pushing a cleaning cart that contained several more supplies than cleaning products, I carried myself down the hall. Making my way to the second floor using the elevator, I began snooping. Standing in a long corridor and pushing my cart, I began trying closed doors. Damn, so many locked doors, none of which triggered any genuine interest in me. Pushing on every door all the way to the elevator, some had engraved nameplates on the doors, but most did not.

Entering the elevator, I stared at the floors highlighted on the panel. I don't have all night. Pushing number twelve, the top floor, I waited to see if it would be that easy. No such luck. The elevator simply didn't move. Ok, sucking in then biting my lips, I thought, what the hell, and I tried floor eleven, and the doors closed with cooperation. Not understanding what to expect, I just rode along. The door slid open, and I pushed my cart out. My eyes popped out of their sockets with bright pink colors on the walls. Cheery rainbow-colored balloons were painted on the walls to add a feeling of joy to the scene portrayed. Looking up, I read the sky blue painted sign to read Maternity Ward. Well, I thought, this is one of the stops I planned for. As I pushed my cart along, I peered into several glass rooms and observed women in different stages of pregnancy.

The rooms were all furnished alike, with a full-sized bed, a large overstuffed chair, a small table for one and a screen. Peering in at the women, I stood there gazing at many sleeping women before I noticed they didn't look up at me. I don't think they could see through the window clearly, because no one looked up to acknowledge me. Were they here of their own volition? Are they being harmed? I grabbed my pregnant costume and dipped into the bathroom. I dropped a short, loose-fitting dress over the top of the costume. In the distance, I could have sworn I heard a dog bark. But that couldn't be right. Choosing a girl at random, I wanted to question her welfare. Trying the door handle, it turned easily. I quickly slipped inside and shut the door behind me.

The young woman jumped at my entry and let out a squeal. She grabbed her chest and screamed, "Who are you and what do you want!" Her gaze lingered on my fake pregnancy belly, then looked up at my eyes. The woman had dark skin, shoulder-length black curly hair, large brown eyes and huge breasts that were loose inside a thin nightgown. "Bored," was what I blurted out because I couldn't think of another answer. *I sure didn't think this part out thoroughly*, I thought. Her eyes squinted in speculation. "Well, you need to return to your room. You ought to know by now no visiting, so leave!" Frustrated, I responded, "I will, just wondering if Ricky M is the father of your baby as well." Rubbing my belly for effect, I stared at her. Her eyebrows drew up to her hairline.

Her agitation was clear. She asked, "Are you insane? My husband and I are having this child." Her eyes grew glassy, and her face dropped all emotion. Her lips opened, then her mouth, and out came a dry voice that was hers but not. She said, "Ricky M is a great man. He has found me an improved husband. Now I can have several children." She smiled, and her expression returned to the one she possessed when I entered. Quickly it shifted to rage, and she shouted, "Get back to your room, you crazy woman, before I call security!"

I turned to leave. Obviously, I wasn't getting any more from the woman. As soon as I got out of her room, I could hear dogs barking at a distance. So weird, I thought. Starting to change out of the big belly pregnancy costume, I heard a loud buzzing noise and some muffled warning. I may need to make a break for it, so I threw the gown I was wearing back on. Just as soon as I got outside the bathroom, I could make out an announcement booming through the halls, just as the door shut behind me. A male voice, still at a distance, says, "Floor eleven lockdown. Hounds on patrol in fifteen minutes". Oh no, I thought, guards who keep dogs in the building? Nothing I have in my cleaning cart will help. Panic seized me. Think, I said to myself.

The barking began as it grew closer by the minute. Looking at myself still dressed in a gown, should I change back into the maid uniform and try to bluff my way out? I can't think of a partially legitimate reason to be up here, several floors away from where I started. Do I gamble my voice influence will work, but what about the dogs? Looking around, I finally let my mind calm enough to see a potential escape opportunity without confrontation. A vent large enough for to let me squeeze into it. Now I can hear the click of claws on the polished floor. Decision made. My chances of going to jail for trespassing are probably greater if I try talking the guards into some story.

My voice may work, but the dogs worry me. Rushing to my cart, I retrieved my tools and opened the vent. I backed myself inside, feet first, and replaced the vent cover. It hit me that the vent was not quite large enough for me to crawl on all fours. My only recourse was to enter backward. Therefore, I levered myself so that I could go inside. Once I did, I started scooting backward through the vent. The dogs reached the vent just as I backed up enough that they were not visible to me. Radio's clicks were echoing through the vent.

The dogs were so loud I couldn't make anything out. My adrenaline was pumping, and I was moving as fast as I could. Finally, the barking sounds faded, and I could let out the breath I was holding. My beating heart was returning to normal until I had a flashback of being trapped in a vent. Trying to push the memories down failed, and it was like I was seeing and feeling my past. Breathing through my constricting lungs was difficult. My heating body and my vision were drawing down to a small thin string of light. My wants and needs became only one thing, fear I have to get out.

Rational thought was gone, I began banging out with my hands and bucking inside the trapped vent. Bucking my hips up and down, I could barely suppress a scream. Only a small part of my logical brain was still functioning. Still wearing only a short dress and panties, it felt like bugs crawling over my skin, and I couldn't bend my head to look down. Next, I fell. The ceiling had given way, and there was no time to brace for impact. The lights went out, all sounds went out, and my body exploded with pain. My first thought was, did I lose consciousness? There was no way to tell, as at first, the sounds flooded my ears of hissing cats. What the hell? Why am I covered in slime? My vision cleared, and the pain was fading. Sitting up, I looked around to find myself in some kind of kennel for cats. I was laying in the middle of a cage covered in blood and other things. Gaining my feet, I used a squat walk to the exit of the cage. Looking around the space, I recognized this to be a lab.

Despite my prior knowledge of the DNA extraction from various animals to create the trendy drugs that transformed young adults into their animal personalities, I had never imagined the caged animals with tubes of fluids coursing through their bodies. Not fairing well myself, I looked down to see the various scratches and bites I received from the animals. Maybe I was out for a few minutes. I went to access the computer, hoping to determine my location and get out. Touching the screen brought the computer to life and, just as I feared, it was password locked.

Now what? I mean, I got some decent hacking skills, but on the level needed to break this computer was not in my skill set. Still staring at the computer, I saw the camera light come on, and before I could process this, it was off again. Frowning at the camera, I wondered if I had even seen it. My eyes caught a change in the screen, and the password lock shifted to unlock. Ok, I will not think about this much. Within a few minutes, I pulled up the menu, then the schematic of the building. Right there, marked in red, was Ricky M's office. This is what I was looking for, and I studied its location. I am on the maternity ward.

This includes the animals. Now I see clearly I'm in the feline section. My panic attack landed me at the rear end of the building. Guessing I would say this is where they milk the DNA out of the young felines. Looking at my naked body, it occurred to me some DNA may have seeped into my myriad of scrapes and punctures. This was, again, something to push into the back of my mind. Now let me find some dirt on Ricky M. I open the window that was labeled company memos. Suddenly an angry red "Access Denied, shut down."

That was all I was going to get. I carefully picked multiple bits of debris off my skin while I contemplated my next move to exit. It was disturbing. A needle with a tube attached was still pumping fluid from an unmarked bag into the underside of my thigh. Why I didn't initially see it, I don't know. Although it sickened me to think about that thing pumping fluid inside of me, I had no time to dwell on this. I yanked it out. Creeping to the door, I peered out to see the corridor was clear. I padded down the hall, found the stairwell, and crept down to the first floor. Standing near the elevator was a guard facing the outside door.

My movement must have alerted him, and this tall, fully armed man with a hangdog face approached me. When he was within ten feet, he sniffed the air while his eyes bored into me. Having nothing to lose, I put as much base in my voice as I could. I said, "Take me to the exit and lead me out of here." His hand snaked out and grabbed mine. Flight popped into my brain, but I wanted to see what he would do. He led me out the door. Once in the parking lot, he turned and walked back inside. Well, that confirms my voice influence works well here. That is definitively a boon I will use when I return for Ricky M.

Chapter 10
Phase III plan

A few days later, Mrs. Miller sent me the documented proof of Ricky M's illegal doing on a drive. The separation of marital partners was distasteful, but not illegal. Ricky's orgy parties fell into the same category. However, the business run by Sandy that appeared to perform Invitro pregnancies did a lot more. This is where the extortion part of the company lived. They were drugging men into rape, then blackmailing them into giving up their genetic material. Putting a stop to this and revenge dominated all my thoughts, no one could sway me from my desires.

Today is the day I begin the last phase of my revenge. Most of all, I would get the answers to why? Now that I have friends, I informed them of the plan and when I would go. If successful, I would come out as the head of the company, and the illegal and distasteful stuff would end. Rising this morning, I had a genuine smile on my face. The first I wore since I was with my Shane. Dressing in front of the mirror, I carefully applied makeup, then put my locks into a top bun. I added earrings and, lastly, black pumps. Staring at myself, I thought, *this is the day I take everything from him like he did me.*

I Strategically Parked My Car Half a Mile from the Corporation's Gates! I strolled up to the gate with confidence, as planned, the guards got my voice and scent better at the entrance to the building. Then I strode in like I was the second coming. I said, "Let me see Ricky M." They got that same look as those guys at Mrs. Miller's house and stood aside and pointed to the main door. I walked up to the front desk and asked for the code to the elevator, so I could access the top floor suite. The executive at the desk was an attractive man, about 5'9 with a short crop of brown hair and sky-blue eyes, who looked at me as like he was star struck. I loved it. He obeyed my command, and I stepped into the elevator. The butterflies were leaping in my belly. I had this, I told myself and put the smuggest look on my face I had. I stepped out of the elevator and was a little worried.

If the executive assistant were a woman, everything would be lost. What chaos I would need to create, but again it was a male and relief soothed my nerves. Yes, I walked up and asked if Ricky M was in his office. His face scrunched up like he was in pain. Oh no, I thought, my power over him was weak. He asked while wearing a constipated look.

"Who are you and why are you here?" Panic seized me, then I remembered the small spray bottle in my pocket that contained my menstrual blood. Spraying him in the face, I hoped for a quick reaction. Moments later, his face changed from being confused to fury, then finally into that blank look the others had. The man acknowledged me and turned to show me the office. I said with the all the air of authority I could fake, "Hold his calls and appointments." The man, whose nameplate on his desk read Ronald, acknowledged me and returned to what he was doing. Here we go, I thought. I put my game face on. I strutted through the door and shut it behind me. Looking around the office, I found it wasn't as impressive as I thought it might be. The room was enormous, that was true but sparsely decorated. A large desk backed up against the wall, set on plush beige carpeting. My eyes zeroed in on the man behind the desk. Ricky M didn't notice anyone had entered at first. He was seated while manipulating multiple holographic screens in front of him. I sucked in a deep breath and began the mantra I had rehearsed in my head dozens of times already.

"Ricky M, have you had enough of my toying with you like you do with the lives of others around you? You killed my husband and two other men I know. I am going to take all this from you." The most confident smile I had been mine. I waved my hands to show this building. My voice was ready to project my next words to command his obedience as I opened my mouth. "Stand up," I said. Ricky M's intense staring at me was a little disheartening. His eyes grew larger by the moment. The large nostrils on his snout like nose flared as it took in my scent, just like I had hoped. Now he will have to heel to my command, I knew. He stood to his full height. I must admit, he sure looked taller by about two or three inches than I last saw him in my bedroom. That is impossible, right? Within a blink of my eye, he crouched again. He planted his hands firmly on the desk. Then, before I inhaled to take my next breath, he leaped over his desk. By my inhale, he had covered the distance between us of about ten feet. Impossible. I had no time to react before his hands were on my throat, squeezing. There was no air, and he was so strong. I couldn't move. I grasped his hands, attempting to break his hold. There was no breaking that vice-like grip. His face was so close to mine that if I could take in air, it would come from him. I couldn't do anything, especially the most important thing, breathing. He smiled in my face while my mouth gaped open, trying to grab oxygen. Darkness was encroaching from the edges of my vision. My lungs were burning, and I was dying. This is how it ends, really? I'm not ready.

I barely felt it when he shoved something in my mouth, damn near down my throat. He released his hand on my throat, and I swallowed before trying. I took a breath of air. As I took in oxygen, I leaned over with my hands on my knees and was gasping for air. There was no time to even look for where Ricky M was now. I just needed air. While I was practically hacking up a lung in a coughing fit, a bottle of some liquid thrust into my face was my saving grace. Under other circumstances, I may have refused, if my brain was working, but it wasn't, so I guzzled it down. It didn't taste unusual, but what did I know? I put my hand on the wall for support while I tried to gather my wits. Then I got angry and coughed out, "What the hell did you force on me?" In a barely-speaking mouth, it seemed like there were more teeth than a regular human mouth should have. He said, "Something to help you relax. We need to negotiate, don't you think?" I turned my body to project strength and looked at him, all three of him. No, maybe he is fading in and out. There are pretty little stars and birds flying around his head. The room started fading in and out and spun, then it all went dark.

I came to consciousness and to find myself on my back, my eyes were still closed, and I can hear a gentle music playing. My muddled mind was waking from a hangover, and I do not know where I am. Opening my eyes is a struggle. They must have two ton weights, but Shane is licking me. I feel the wet tongue diving inside my body between my legs. We must be home and safe.

We rarely have oral sex this way, but if we are, then we must be in a good place. But why did I pass out? That is unlike me. Why hasn't he noticed? Shane's ministrations feel good, so I groan. I think Shane has never been that noisy about it. Today, he sounds like he is slurping milk or something. I giggle and try again to open my eyes while reaching down with my hands to feel his hair. His hair feels very different. Something is wrong. The sounds and smells around me are off. This realization and panic helped me push through the weights and my eyes sprung open. I looked at an unfamiliar white ceiling, a white wall again and no decoration. My eyes drifted further down the top of the head of a sandy short-haired man, definitely not my Shane. Then his facelifts, and it is the canine like face of a man I can't recall who. The shock and horror hit me that this was not Shane. Where is Shane? Where am I? Just as I screamed, he raised himself to a seated position. Staring at me for a moment with piercing eyes, he puts his big hand on my mouth. "My dear Rachel, you are still not ready to be more reasonable."

He removes his hand and pulls a syringe from nowhere with the other. My mind didn't catch up with what was happening before he injected me into my inner thigh, and everything went dark again. A time later, I opened my eyes, and I was lying on the floor on top of something thick and fluffy. My head was on the chest of a strange hard male body, that was stroking my naked body from my breasts down and between my legs. My brain was foggy, but I knew this wasn't. Wait, who was I trying to remember? I glanced around the room. I think it was totally different front the one I woke up to earlier. Sparsely furnished, the room was nothing special, except there was no obvious door allowing a way out.

I could see a large wooden desk that was backed against a wall. Just above it was a tiny window. A small round table, with two chairs on each side, sat about ¾'s length of the room away from the desk. Next, a leather couch was located on the opposite side of the room from the desk, backed against the wall, was smooth and appeared seamless. That's when I noticed there were no breaks in the walls except for when it bent around corners, not even a door. Why did I think about escaping? Did I need to escape? What is wrong with me? I can't even remember where or who I am. Trying to get my bearings, I began looking around. There was a sofa with a coffee table, a kitchen table with two chairs against it, and what appeared to be a small bathroom. I lifted my head to look at the man stroking me in such a familiar way. He was smiling like I should know him. He looked familiar, but my brain couldn't place him. I opened my mouth to question the man, and my voice sounded strange to me. Or maybe I always sound like this. The man smiled so warmly at me and said, "You are my mate. We were born to be together, and now we are."

It felt good to be held in his arms, and I snuggled down. That unfamiliar sounding voice came out of me when I spoke again, "How come I don't remember? What is your name? What is my name? I panicked and tried to break free of him." He restrained me and said, "Calm down and relax, Rachel. Your memory will come back to you in a couple of hours. You know me," he spoke so reassuringly. "I am Ricky M. You came here to talk to me about how we are going to start our lives together. Just take a deep breath, and you will recognize my pheromones, just like I know yours. I had to give you a DNA booster to help you realize what I have known for some time, that we are mates." His eyes scanned my face Intensely. "I have been looking for my pheromone match for years now. You are unique. Your body was already producing in a small amount of the natural pheromone scent to enhance the male's physical desire. Like myself, you're altered by Long COVID to have an influential voice. All this, combined with the DNA enhancements I have given, makes your body one of the billions in its uniqueness.

You are my perfect match." I sat up and looked at myself. There were marks on my arms. I looked like a junkie with track marks. I continued to examine myself and the bruising between my legs. What the hell has happened to me, and how long have I been here? However, I asked the most relevant question first. "Did you do this to me? I pointed to the marks on my arms. Why am I naked?" Noting he was naked as well. I tried to sit up again and again, but he restrained me. I only had the freedom to move part of my upper body.

He was in total control. This I understand, so I need to acknowledge and act accordingly until I see an opening to do otherwise. So I asked the next obvious question, "Did we have sex?" Ricky laughed, "Not yet. I needed to taste you to make sure I firmly have you inside me. I frowned in disgust. He continued, when you are around others, I can dampen the impact of your pheromones on others." I didn't understand that at all. This sounds crazy, but my mind is still off, so I will let that go. Then my most recent memory rushed back like being hit with a brick wall.

I shuttered and cried out, "You choked me!" He said, "I would never truly hurt you, but you were misguided and out of control. You wouldn't even listen to reason. I took action, so we could be like this, our true selves.

Do you think you can stand now?" He asked as though this entire conversation was like an everyday thing. With no argument in mind, I nodded and went along. For now, my mind swam with a confused, jumble of thoughts. We both stood as he guided me to a sofa that was placed against the wall. He was about my height, a well-built, attractive white man. He had a lot more hair all over his body than my tastes usually go toward, but he definitely had other attractive packages. When we sat, I heard a hissing, a sound. I looked around for the source, but didn't find it. He asked, "So, what did you come to ask me?" I thought long and hard. I know I had a plan, but my thoughts were still confused. His hair looks so soft. I wonder what it feels like? Oh, no, not him, he is the enemy, was screaming in my head, but I can't remember why. Slowly, the scream was becoming a whisper, soon nonexistent. His face changed into something familiar and trusting. His blue eyes sparkled as they reflected the affection he had for me. He told me I was his mate. I wondered what does that mean. It feels good? He holds my hand and looks at me like I belong to him. Is this true? His chest is just right there for me to touch. I remember the sensations between my legs. He was licking me there while I was scared and trying to scream. Why would I scream? I dismissed the thought and fixed it on his hair. I can't help myself. He has hair that I find irresistible, and I run my hand through it. He takes that as permission to kiss my shoulder, neck, and cheek. Ricky whispered in my ear while gently nibbling. "My research that launched my corporation with Tran species groups was really my research into finding one's true mate. Using a combination of DNA from different animal species, I found that healthy women formally unable to conceive could have healthy babies.

All I needed to do was find the right combinations in a male. Once I have a potential match, I arrange to have all the parties meet up at one of my homes to see if they can detect the desired pheromones of their partner. Then it is done, and a new match is made that would produce offspring, just as nature intended. However, some people like me are so unique that it didn't work until one of my clinics found you." He offered no more explanation as I groaned with pleasure and saw no reason to stop his ministrations. He kept kissing me until he got to my lips and I open to let him in. The snout was awkward, but his tongue was very long. His hands are on my breasts and mine on his. He is pinching and rolling. His mouth leaves mine and is on my nipples. I put my head back. Taking that opportunity to push me down, so that he is laying on top. He splits my legs with his body, and I can feel how hard he is. He pulls away from my breasts and says, "Rachel, you weren't told the truth.

I wanted to be the man you have children with. The first time I saw your DNA profile, I knew you were for me. You weren't ready, and I tried to convince you. Truly, I have the best interest of mankind at heart. You and I will be the Adam and Eve or the King and Queen of my plantation." My mind whirled with fragments of half formed thoughts, and faces of people I should know swam in those fragments. Concentration was becoming difficult as I became quite tired, although he was still massaging my body. My eyes were heavy, and all went dark without me uttering another word.

Aussie Enters The World

Chapter 11
A dog's life with the birth of Number 2

Thump, Thump, Whoosh...

Silence and darkness all around me. I just entered a new world. What's this I feel that makes me shiver? Oh, cold! The loud, familiar thumping is gone, and the darkness remains. Oh, now I feel good. I hear that familiar voice in my head. "Come to me, my sweet boy. I will feed and warm you." She moves me closer to her and warmth envelops me. What is this? It is so good. The feeding one is soft and warm and there is that sound again. Thump, Thump, Thump, it feels comfortable. My tummy is now full, and I'm so sleepy. "Just sleep now with your pack mates, my boy." Oh, I thought my mates felt soft, and I liked being next to them in a pile.

My tummy grumbles again. I reach out with my face and the Feeder plops the warm yummy liquid from her body into my mouth. I hear a giggle. "Number 2, I am your mommy, not your feeder." I began squirming around in the darkness, until I find a warm, comfortable spot. I hear Mommy's voice again. " I will take care of you until you can get a pack of your own." The lick of tongue cleaning me was warm and made me tingle. I especially love it when it glides over my belly and behind my ears. "Why can't I be with you always?" I asked while she was finishing up. Mommy just giggled as she finished. The heat of her breath on my fur made me relax and feel so good. Right before I drifted off to sleep, Mommy said, "One day, you will go to join a pack of your own. My Alpha has improved your body, and you and your mates, will be smarter than all before you. I don't know what the two legged Alpha has in store for you, but it will be wonderful. I want you to be strong and smart. This will make me proud." I became tired once again and found a soft place on top of one of my mates and was soon fast asleep.

Each day was similar. I woke, ate and squirmed around my pack, then repeat. One day daylight illuminated around me. At first, the sight was fuzzy, but then I could see a face. Mommy smiled, "Hello, my number 2. Welcome to the world. Meet your pack." Glancing around, there were others like me, not big like my mommy. Their eyes were closed, and they were moving around blindly. Mommy's voice once again rang out, "The two legged's will become your pack. Your job will be to teach and take care of them. She laughed when she said, just make them believe it is their idea. My Alpha has made us, unlike any others of our kind. I will teach you a way to talk to Alpha with your paws like I can. Just eat, sleep and gain your strength. When your pack mates can see, I will teach you. Our Alpha will teach you all kinds of wonderful things. Just do as he asks."

Jack

Forcing my heavy-lidded eyes open, I took stock of my situation. We were once again lying on the enormous bed, and I was in his arms as he stroked my body. I had no sense of time. Raising my head off an impressively muscled chest, I looked at the slit of a window and saw only darkness outside of it. What day was it? The drug was wearing off finally and my memories were coming back in fits. I need something to stimulate myself, so I can think clearly. I looked at Ricky M and asked if I could take a shower. He looked apprehensive. I could see the war raging in his head for the first time. He finally answered and said, "Sure, we can take a shower together." Did I want to shower with him? No, I don't think so, or maybe I do? My scrambled thoughts feel like trying to catch a cloud. For a moment, I held the thought that I rarely did that with another person, not even my..., then I lost the thought. The drugs were still in my system, and it felt like cotton between my ears. I almost remembered someone or something important. I smiled and said, "Great, let's take a shower." Ricky told me my memories would return within hours after he administered whatever drugs he used, but I feel it has been much longer than mere hours. He held my hand as we walked to the bathroom. Feeling awkward in the small space and panic rising, but his hand helped me push it down. Ricky M hardly let me make a move without him. Even when I reached outside the shower for a towel, he looked as though he might panic.

I was very suspicious, but acted as though I didn't notice. What is he afraid of? I must remember to find out? He said my memory is returning. Does he think I will reject him? Will I? His smell is so good to me? I wanted so much to rub myself against him, but I restrained myself. Ricky's eyes roamed every corner of my body as I lathered and rinsed off. Lustily, he said, "I've kept up with all your movements for several months now. No pictures do your body justice." He appeared to have a hard time restraining himself, but he only let his hand glide down my arm to my hips before removing it. It wasn't unpleasant, but it felt wrong on some level. I hurriedly finished my shower and reached for the door to step out.

When I stepped outside his bathroom, there was a scrumptious breakfast spread placed on the table of the adjacent room. Wow, was I in the shower that long? Is it already morning, and what day is it? How can I tell day or night? Looking up at the small windows gave me no clue as to what day is it. Now the sun's rays of dawn were breaking through. I saw the panic again flash in Ricky M's eyes. Moments later, a warm smile crossed his face. I wondered what. I only looked at the window but said nothing. He removed my towel and threw it onto the floor of the bathroom. Standing there naked, his eyes roamed over my body. All I could do was wrap my arms around myself.

He said in a husky voice, "I prefer you this way, all natural as you were. No matter how old you are or plump your body becomes, once it is rounded with my children, I will never stop wanted you." Putting his hands on my hips and bringing my body toward him, he kissed me with such lust, he stirred cravings inside me. His tongue entered my mouth and his hands caressed my hips. His scent was becoming more than familiar to me, and all my questions once again faded into the background. Pulling away from me, I watched as he fisted his large manhood. A pearly drop came to the head. He took the drop of the pre-cum and smeared the ejaculation on my face, under my nose, onto my lips and inside my mouth. I jumped back, or at least tried to. Ricky's hand snaked out lightning fast and restrained me in place with his other hand. With his eyes boring into me as though he was waiting for something to happen. It was not something I was expecting or would have wanted, but the scent and taste of him was overwhelming. I knew he was my man, my mate, and my acceptance was not an option. Now I know why I am attracted to him. We are mates. Because of the animal DNA, my attraction is on a cellular level. Why, some animals mate for life, I thought. Aware he has injected something inside of me and I have no ability to do anything about it. I just went with my instincts. Now my instincts and body recognize him as my mate, but my mind feels I have a choice. His fierce look turned to pure joy. He all but shouted, "I knew you were the one. Only my true mate would respond to my seed. I can no more be without you than you can me." I looked at him and said, "Mate? How long, are we mates for life?" His hand left the restraint on my hips and reached down in between my legs to part them. I let out a gasp when he thrust an index finger into my wetness. Staring at me all the while, he pulled it out just as suddenly and placed it in his mouth. Groaning out in pleasure, he said, "Your taste is inside me and is the only one that will ever be there. You will have my children, and we will live for many years together." He looked at me, and finally seemed to relax, like my acceptance meant his life can begin. Do I really accept this? No, but my thoughts and feelings are so disjointed, I can only use my instincts. Ricky M turned to the table set with the breakfast foods. Through all that, that he just did, I have forgotten the food that was sitting on a small table a few feet from us. The food smell hit me like a bullet, and my stomach grumbled as though it had never been fed before. It all looked so good that I grinned like a starving woman. It took everything I had not to fall on the food like a rabid animal. His lips were turned up into a smile again and he said, "This is the first of many meals we will share together." Crazy me, I found I really liked his smile as we sat. Ricky M looked at his breakfast. A frown crept over his face. He said, "Strawberry Crêpes, I don't care for these; they know this. I was still smiling when I looked at mine. But I'm glad you appear to not feel the same about them. I will eat them anyway." He smiled. He took a sip of his coffee as I watched. Looking at my food, I had a flash of a smiling face of a beautiful brown-skinned woman with bright strawberry hair. I was trying hard to hold on to the memory, but I lost it like sand through my fingers. Cutting my delicious looking strawberry crêpe, I popped a piece into my mouth. It was absolutely delicious, I moaned with delight. All the dishes and food on the table rocked. For a moment, I considered there must be an earthquake. But wait, we don't have earthquakes on the East Coast. My gaze flipped up to see Ricky M staring at me with lust in his eyes, while his hands were white-knuckle gripping the table on its sides. He said, "On second thought, if you keep making that sound, I think I will make sure this is on the menu more often." I took a sip of hot tea with cream and looked into my cup. The cream had a big shape of a 'S' like a name I am trying to remember. "Can I ask you a few questions?" I asked while placing another mouthful of Crêpes on my fork and bringing it to my mouth, then licking my lips. I saw Ricky M's eyes following my fork to my lips, then fixing there. Now Ricky M's white-knuckle grip on the table hadn't relented, as he looked like he was barely holding himself together. I took this as my cue. "Why am I your mate and prisoner? Is it some 'Handmaids' stuff?" I put a mouthful of strawberry dripping in syrup in my mouth. He was so entranced as I chewed that I think he couldn't help but answer honestly. He spoke in a monologue voice, "No, I learned that some women between ages 18 & 40 years old never conceive children because they never have the right mate. Using my DNA enhancement, men can use scent to discover the right woman. Once I meet with them, I convince them this is the right match for them. Mated with the correct partner, the two can conceive children as they are meant to. My problem is that I have not found until now that match for myself until now. Then, when I did, she kept running from me." He smiled a self-deprecating smile when he said, "You wouldn't give me a chance to explain what we could be together. When I saw the results of your last doctor's lab tests, I read your background file. I found you had the same long COVID I had, as well as several other compatible factors. When you couldn't conceive with that man you were with, I knew it was because you were mine, but I couldn't persuade you or him of my wisdom.

"What, man?" I asked just as some syrup dropped from the corner of my mouth and I licked at it with my tongue. Just then, I felt the table and dishes upend and all were sailing into the air. I looked up back down at him or where he was, but his chair was empty. What the hell? I thought. My head swiveled around to search for him, when my legs felt like they were pulled from under me and my butt landed on the floor. He was between my legs, licking and gently biting. He was so intent on his goal and my disorientation so complete I never heard all the dishes crash to the floor. I grabbed the top of his head and initially tried to stop him, but our combined scents created a burst of pleasure that overtook me. Just when an orgasm began, his head was gone, and he lifted me off the floor and while tossing me onto the bed, with such a quick motion, it left me dizzy. He was suddenly kneeling before me, in between my legs. His manhood was long, thick, and posed to enter me. As sudden as before, he slid backward off the bed and moved so quickly my eyes couldn't keep up. Now he was on the bed again and positioned so that his penis was on my face. I had no time to react. He pinched my jaws, forcing my mouth open, then he shoved himself inside. I was not unfamiliar with this position, and finding I had little choice, I got into it. He must have enjoyed it, because I heard his groans and some barks or howls of pleasure. Just when I was prepared for the explosion of his release, he said something unintelligible under his breath with a groan. Moments later, loudly, he said, "You are almost there, but I can't waste it." Before I could react or question, he snatched himself out of my mouth and turned my body, forced me on my knees and plunged himself into me. He rocked inside me slowly for a few pumps, then drove harder as he got a rhythm. Breathless and with some effort, he said, "I want to explain everything to you, but you aren't ready. Taking a few more heavy breaths before he continued, "I just can't wait until the bond between us is at full strength" He pumped harder and faster, then I could feel him swell inside me. I never felt a man swell like that before, and I tried to pull back, so he would come out. Then something happened that I still am unsure of the how and why. My body clenched up as well, not with orgasm, but something more. In my fear, I tried again to pull away to get him out of me, but we were stuck. He howled like an injured animal, as though it hurt him, and he couldn't withdraw. I stopped trying. He gripped my hips tighter and made a growling noise that made me settle and obey. Still, I am unsure of why that sound forced my obedience. Within moments, he howled with his explosion of a release. Feeling the warmth of his spray inside me, I achieved another orgasm. I knew something changed. I could smell a difference. He took a long sniff as well. We both fell on our sides to the bed, and we were still locked, with his hands wrapped around my waist. He breathed into my ear, and he nibbled and kissed my neck. His voice had pure joy in its sound, saying, "We created life." Now, I am not sure what was going on but incredible sex, but I'm sure he has lost his mind. We lay there in silence. He kissed my shoulders and the side of my face, leaving me with no more information. Memories flashed in my mind of a familiar face, smiling. It was someone I knew, and he looked at me with love. The next I saw him, he was dead, and I was throwing dirt on his body. My heart was breaking. It was all my fault. His life was too short. I took a deep inhale, then all my memories came roaring back, and I remembered everything. I came here for many reasons but foremost was revenge for Ricky's part in Shane's death. Sex with him was good, but not enough for me to want anything else to do with this man. He was right about one thing; however, once he spread his seed under my nose, I knew I was his mate. There are mating laws in several states, and both North and South Carolina are included. They are clear. If ever challenged, he would be able to prove we are mates. These laws, while similar to a marriage contract, they have differences. He can't force me to live with him, but he has rights over whom I can have sex with and our children. That's a bridge I would deal with when I have to cross it. Right now, my mind started spinning on how to escape my current predicament. Right now, I am literally stuck.

Finally, after about twenty minutes, my muscles relaxed and his penis came out. The fluids that came out were on us more than I had ever seen before. I really wanted to rinse him off of me. I sucked up my anger, turned to Ricky M and said, "Shouldn't we go to the shower and clean up, then maybe put clothes on?" He said, "You know, don't you? What has happened?" He sat up, then pulled me onto his lap. It was like a gallon of fluids poured out of us and even dripping on the floor. It was disgusting. However, he didn't seem bothered. How could he know I remembered everything? I let this play out. He was so pleased with himself and continued, "I know your mind is clearing. I will answer all of your questions, and you will wear clothes again soon. I must admit, I would be just as happy if you never wore clothes again." He was really reaching my threshold of too much creeping me out. I tried to pull away from him, saying, "I have to use the bathroom." He still held me longer, finally letting his fingers loosen his grip, but then he got up with me and followed me. "Am I a prisoner?" I was afraid for the first time. I shouldn't be here, I thought. This is wrong. He read the fear on my face. "You are my mate, not a prisoner. It's just your conversion made you not so steady. I don't want you to hurt yourself. "Conversion?" I asked while walking because the urgency to pee was increasing so much that I ran. He beat me to the bathroom, opened the door, and stood inside while I went to sit. If I hadn't had to go so badly, I wouldn't have been able to release my bladder with him there, but I let it all go. He again looked at my body with that transfixed look. "May I shower?" I asked, while looking up from the toilet. He said, "No, please don't do that. I like that feisty temper of yours. I know you are afraid. Try to accept things for now without changing who you are. I love who you are." I stood and waited for his permission. He looked irritated, and turned his back to walk out. This showed me that I could shower. Now I have another way to needle him. I must collect ways to irritate him to find a way out. I know I will need to get out of here, whether it be by escape or death. I will hope for the prior, but if it takes the ladder, then I accept that too.

Chapter 12
Now, the insanity begins

I took a long shower, so long that Ricky came back into then out of the bathroom several times before giving up. That was good. I wiped the mirror of condensation, toweled off, and looked at myself. My appearance had changed. My face was elongating, my eyes were larger with thicker lashes, and I had longer canine teeth. As bad as that was, my hair was awful, which is the thing that bothered me most. I suspect I have been here for more than a few days, judging by the fact my hair twists are loose and look worse than a rat's nest on my head.

I do not know what Ricky M has drugged me with or how often, but I feel different. Right now, all I can do is play along, making him let down his guard all the while. I will gather intel and wait for my time to escape. This is just like the foster homes before my last home, with me just biding my time.

The next morning, or at least I assume so because of the meal. There were delicious-looking blueberry pancakes, scrambled eggs and sausage links. Besides a tall cup of orange juice sat a pill bottle with my name on it. Clearly written in a large black print read: Rachel Monroe, Prenatal vitamins. "*Oh My God,* I thought, *this guy really believes I am pregnant after one time of sex.*" My eyes rose to him. He wore a smug look as though he was proud of his potency. There was no way to fight him, so I opened the bottle and washed it down with my juice.

The self-satisfied grin remained as he picked up his fork and stared at his eggs. I did the same thing every day after that. The pills were waiting for me. At least it gave me some sense of time. After we had eaten, I got up and walked into the bathroom. He followed me as though I was going to do something other than pee. Eyeing him the whole time, I flopped on the toilet seat and released my urine. Then, stood and washed my hands, jerking me away from the sink. He wrapped me in his arms.

Kissing me passionately, he pulled me to the tub. Insisting we take a bath together, he lifted me to adjust me in the tub. His back was against the back of the tub and mine was to his front. Pouring water over my shoulders first, he added soap to wash my back. After a few minutes, he got out, toweled off and left the bathroom, allowing me to soak. I languished there for several minutes before finally leaving.

I walked out of the bathroom and 'my mate' was sitting on the sofa waiting. Still unseen hands had cleared the breakfast away, and he had a flowery dress laid across his nude lap. Wow, I thought, he certainly has no problem with nudity, and I am just realizing my discomfort with it. I smiled and said, "Well, I'm sure that would look very nice on you. Are you going to model it for your mate?" He laughed, and it was a delightful laugh. I genuinely laughed as well. He held it out to me. "A peace offering. I want us to clear the air between each other." I took the dress and kissed him on the lips. "Thank you," I said while I slipped the dress over my head. Then, he spun around for his approval.

Grinning, he put his arms around my waist and then moved them to rest on my belly. He fixed that smile I couldn't place on his face as his eyes left my flat belly to look me in the eyes. Using his considerable speed and strength, he just pulled me to his lap and held me without speaking for a while. That strange hissing sound started again from somewhere behind the sofa. It resembled the sound a motor makes when starting up. I suspect this is some gas that he is using to drugging me. With no idea what it is doing to me, I can only speculate. I keep waking up lying on his chest, so I never wake where I sleep.

My guess is he is using this time to do something to me or to leave the room unseen. Interrupting my thoughts, he said, "OK, Rachel, let me explain why we are here?" I was going to say my name is Jack, but just then, the sun hit his eyes just right, and I saw the contacts in them. The puzzle pieces slid into place. I could see a flash of the digital readout in them. For only a moment, that was enough for me to know what they were.

Now I understand why I see nobody. He is remotely controlling this environment with digital contacts. He is monitoring the gas, the shower, the food delivery, the clothes, the bedding, and he changes everything. Not letting on to my discovery, I finished my sentence by raising my hands to rub it through his hair, saying, "The colors in your hair are so amazing. It is so soft and feels good against my skin." This statement pleased him, as it was meant it to, and he stroked my back.

He took a deep breath and let it out. I thought to myself, here comes the lies, and I will have sucked it up like an airhead. Patience and pretending are the way to go when one is in the hands of a captor. After all, I have laid still and taken worse abuse from others. Until I can "Hijack" the situation and turn the tables, I will listen. Whatever drug he was using in the hidden vents calmed me, but my mind was clear and memories were pouring in.

He started his dialogue. I was first alerted by Sandra Beaudreux of the disturbances you caused her. I read the file on your DNA makeup and could see you were a potential candidate for a mate. I asked her about your well-being and why you were attacking her and her subordinate. She explained to me that you had a genetic deposit with the company she runs. She found your husband signed it back to our company, and then she redistributed it. I told her to compensate and keep tabs on you.

I would approach you myself at another time. Much later, I learned the extent of how upset you were about your husband signing away your eggs and holding her responsible. My responsibility for your loss had me wanting you close to me and the slight chance I am your mate. When I saw you on the road, I thought if I offered you a job, I could at least partially make up for the mistake of my business and keep you close. You took my offer the wrong way and ran from me. I guess because you and your friend were gaslighting my employees."

I was slightly amused at how he referred to my husband Shane as my friend, then tossed in the assault on me as a subtle job offer, but I went listened intently. "Then my associate and I came over for a visit to give you a solution to your conception problems. So we injected your lover with the workable solution, but you ran off before it took hold. He had an adverse reaction and had to be restrained for his own good, and we couldn't find you to bring you to him." Amazing, I stared at his face, trying to read if he really believed what he was saying. To my astonishment, I couldn't read the deceit in his face. "Then, months later, you show up and find him on your own in the care of my people. I greeted you kindly, although you broke into my home, and again you ran from me to disappear again. Only to reappear again and to attack and accuse me of some wrongdoing. It turned out your pranks were beneficial on many levels and I had a lot of laughs, so all is well now we are together. Now, we are going to have our own children.

"I almost lost my composure when he said that, but I pulled it together and had to figure out how to phrase my questions. In rapid succession, I asked several of my burning questions. "Why were the other men in your dungeon in your house, and why were they poisoned? Why did you shoot and kill one of them? Why are you running a scam with Sandy and Jessie? Do you have other mates, and what? Why separate the women from their husbands?"

His eyebrows drew together as he looked at me like I was crazy. "Your memory must still be off with the drugs. There were no other men, anyone shot or, for God's sake, a dungeon. There is only one mate. You are the only one that fits the criteria. We are going to have a child in only a few months and will have many more." Ricky M smiled smugly as he held my hands while we sat. I admit I find him attractive, but I can't see myself having real feelings for this misguided man. The men need to find the right women.

The job of repopulating the country falls to all of us." His eyes reflect the look of a man content with his own godhood. It was everything I could do to stop myself from rolling my eyes. Well, now I understand he is using the decline in the U.S. population as his justification for my kidnapping and forced pregnancy. If I am really pregnant. He continued with his insane declaration, "So they can get pregnant and take care of their families, and I will help. The women benefit from the physical enhancements and I guarantee the children will have the best education. I interview the families to ensure no mistreatment regularly.

The DNA enhancements alter the brain's repairing those people that have mental and chemical dependency issues." Smugly, he added, "They just need a little help from me to understand and accept their new partner. Just like you." He must think his voice has persuasion over me, and he can convince me of his truth. Now, I will just wait for my chance to bolt. So I smiled and asked, "Will we live here? What work will I do? I like to work?" Apparent delight was shown on his face as he stood us both up and said, "No, I will soon take you to the mansion. I also know a job for you that suits your unique talents. We need to stay here a few more weeks until I am sure your conversion is complete and verify your pregnancy." Wait what? I exclaimed.

The hissing noise started again, and darkness encroached. I tried to resist, but my eyes were heavy, and I fell asleep.

Once again, I woke with my head lying on his chest and the scent of him in my nose. My first thoughts were my mate, my home. Then, the logical side of my brain kicked in. Just laying there, the wheels in my head were spinning. How come he doesn't pass out each time I do? I wondered. What is he using to block the gas? After all, he is naked? A plan started forming in my head, one I need to know how to tell time and how long I have been here. I need to know how long and how often he puts me to sleep. In order to do that, I need to have a way to track the positions of the sun. Something more precise than holding up my pinching fingers to estimate the light from that tiny window over the desk is poor estimation.

The sparse furniture makes it difficult in here to find another means. I looked around the room and considered my problem. The only other piece of furniture that reflected the sun was a wood desk. That was all that was available for me to use. Ricky M has never let me move toward it or out of his sight long enough to sift through the drawers. I have never seen him over there either, therefore, he could have retrieved nothing from there to inhibit the effect of the gas.

I thought about this issue while Ricky M reminded me we were sitting at the meal table. I could learn the position of the sun on the desk over the next week. Maybe this could help. Ricky asked, "You don't like the Salmon? It is good for the health of the babies." He totally jarred me out of my thoughts with that question. I see we are still in the delusion that, after having sex, he can tell I am pregnant right away. Now with multiples.

Deciding not to entertain this line of conversation right now and get some answers of my own. "I like the food just fine. I was just thinking about where I am. Why, I am your mate, but I am a prisoner as well? Do the other mates hold their mates in the same manner?" I asked while lifting a fork of Salmon to my mouth. His grin fell slightly, but he answered, "No, the other men don't hold their mates prisoner. Once they have completed their conversion, they don't want to leave." He said the last word as though it tasted bitter on his tongue. "It's just you are so feisty. You don't know the whole truth, and I want you to get to know me a little longer before you decide on us." I didn't want to agitate the matter, so I changed the conversation. "Tell me about your family. Are you close? Do you have siblings? He picked up his glass and took a drink, then spoke. I have four siblings and a cousin who acts more like a brother than a cousin. We are all pretty close in age, but there are ego issues between us. My cousin Clifford is the person I that I have to thank for part of the success of my business. He had this idea we would all establish our own plantations."

I stared at him in disbelief. He laughed. "Maybe plantation is an antiquated word. We have territories where we would take care of the people within. Their education, health, and jobs, in return, they and their offspring will support and take care of me for the next hundred years." He rested his eyes on me, waiting for a response that I couldn't find. He wiped his lips with his napkin, looked at my plate and asked If I was done. I just couldn't think past this man is crazy, but on some level enduring. I could only nod. We both got up and went to the sofa. I knew I would sleep soon, so I noted the position of the sun on the desk. I heard a low hiss of something, then drowsiness and nothing.

The smell of Ricky was in my nose when I woke up as I lay on a hard chest. I think I will know his scent anywhere now. I've never given thought to the scent of anyone before unless they were unpleasant. I knew I could track him. This is so much more. I feel a genuine connection to him despite all of what he has done. I remembered my plan and started memorizing the pattern of the day, so I've been out for a couple of hours. Ricky M was again stroking my back and down to my legs. I asked, "Besides carrying your children, what do you want from me?" Ricky M hesitated.

He was probably debating on how much to trust me with. Ricky M turned to his side to look me eye to eye. He kissed my forehead, then my lips tenderly. "You are beautiful. I couldn't have asked for a more beautiful woman. Our children will be perfect. The doctor's confirmation is something I am looking forward to. I didn't want our first time to be so rough. I'm sorry for that. You didn't deserve that. I lost control. You are so beautiful, and I wanted to make love." He kissed me on the lips tenderly. I barely responded. I just didn't see that coming.

Irritated, Ricky M went for another kiss and I gave him the response he wanted, reluctantly. He then did something unexpected. He reached down and squeezed the tip of his penis, got a pearly drop, and rubbed it between his fingers. I watched in bewilderment. Before I could react, he rubbed his fingers under my nose. When the scent hit me, my body reacted and heat pooled between my legs. Moments later, he kissed me again, my reaction was genuine. After sex, again, we lay connected while waiting for my body to release his. This time, he pulled me so that I lay on top of him, a position that was not very comfortable for me, but he seemed to enjoy it.

He stroked my back and said, "I have a confession to make. I ordered Sandy to send your eggs to my Aunt Penny." I wished I could have pulled away from him. However, even if I could, where could I go? I just bit my tongue hard enough to taste my coppery blood in my mouth. He was oblivious and continued. "I ordered Sandy to send some viable eggs combined with the sperm and DNA to my lab. I wanted a child in my cousin's household that I could influence with my voice.

Of course, I did not know until later the uniqueness of your profile. If I had that information in time, I would not have let them get away. Now it is too late. My cousin has gained custody of the child, and we all have an agreement that each of our plantations is sovereign territory. If he knows I want the child, then there is absolutely no chance he would let me see the boy. However, he is subject to my and your influence to a degree. I mean, I couldn't talk him into giving away the child he considers his son. As my mate, you are not welcome in Cliff's plantation without his approval, either. We have to meet, however, annually for our injections to make sure we live for another hundred years. I know this is crazy, but it is true. Cliff created the drug. They set the plantations up to keep us from killing each other over the long span of our lifetimes. I was supposed to have that territory in Maryland. That, however, is another story." I felt my body release him and all the fluids once again flowed all over. He held on to me. I really wanted to get away from him, but he wasn't letting me go. He said, "My brother, Michael." His voice changed into anger. I tried to pull away, and he growled, "Stop trying to get up and listen. "He barked. Turning to him, I looked straight into his bared teeth, black eyes staring daggers at me and withdrawn gums., with his hair standing on end. He looked as though he was ready to bite my head off.

I stopped struggling; my heart was pounding loud enough to be audible, and I trembled. No one has ever provoked that level of fear response in me before. I was a hair away from losing control of my bladder. Maybe he realized the effect he had on me because he suddenly softened his face and released me. "Don't be afraid of me. I could never hurt you." I pulled away and sat on the edge of the bed. He stood and grabbed my hand. "Let's go shower." While we were in the shower, he lathered a washcloth and began washing my back, down my rear, and my legs and spun me around to begin from my chest down. He had a tender smile on his face now. I relaxed. He motioned me to allow him to shampoo and then condition my hair. I never had anyone to do this, and it felt good. Then, a thought struck me. Why had I not considered this before? My hair, which I've done for the past several years, wore a close cut like the typical buzz cut men wear.

Only in the past couple of months did it begin to grow out so that I could put it into twists. I've given no thought to the current length of my hair or my nails. That would give me an idea of how long I've been here. Ricky M asked, "How does that feel?" he rubbed the towel over my formally short crop of hair. I noticed my fingernails were strange-looking. They had indeed grown out with about a couple of weeks of growth.

The appearance was odd. The nail bed looked puffy and thick at the finger joints. I hadn't been awake long enough to truly study myself. My toenails had a similar appearance but darker nails. They were much thicker. I wondered if this was nail fungus or something gross like that. How long have I been here? Will Ricky M. answer the question? Ricky M got out of the shower first, then held a towel open for me to step into.

Chapter 13
Taste of freedom

He removed my towel after drying my body as I walked out of the shower. That was new. I guess he is trying to be more agreeable. He said, "I'm sorry. I don't want to cause you any more stress. I want you to know how unique you are, and I appreciate this. On the wall in front of me was a recording playing. It was of me slithering backward inside a vent.

Next, my body spasming like a crazy woman before crashing into the cat room. Ricky stilled the frame on my fall, with my dress all the up over my shoulders. To my horror, I could see Ricky was staring lustily at my panties and braless breasts. Ricky M had a look of rapture as he spoke, "One of the degrees I earned in school was a Doctorate in Virology. I can assure you your body has unusual changes from a combination of Long COVID sexual contact with your previous husband. After he received Canine DNA injections, you received additional injections in your fall." His eyes drifted off the screen as though he had just remembered the real me standing right beside him.

Even after I confirm the viability of your pregnancy, your hormones will continue to alter your body in ways I can't imagine. I added my own cocktail of injections that will make you more like me, as well as strengthen our children." Smiling like a cat that swallowed the canary while he took a sip of some carbonated drink. He was so pleased with his new toy, Me. as he continued, "I have to remind myself to keep my temper in check so I don't stress you. We want healthy children." I guess that was as close to an apology as I would get for his earlier display, I thought. We walked over to the sofa, and he pulled me onto his lap. Your fall into my feline lab has probably contributed to your uniqueness.

I found some unusual changes in your DNA. I am excited to learn what else you grow into." Trying hard not to let the shock on my face show, all I could do was ask, "You know about that?" A grin appeared on that face that I'm coming to find familiar. Still grinning, he said, "I watched you as you entered the maternity ward, then the feline center. My question is, what happened when you were in the vent to make you freak out?" I kept silent. Additional pictures played me in the maid's clothes, then me in the pregnancy suit. Then, finally, I fell. My dress had slipped up during my fall so that my braless breasts and panties were out there for the world to see. He must have really liked that particular picture because he returned to it a couple more times. Horrified, I turned to him, and he was staring at me. His look was of wonder. "You are absolutely beautiful. I made sure I pulled the footage so I was the only one to see my mate in her glory. By the way, I also let you access the computer. It was not a good idea, but I just wanted to see what you did."

Rubbing and kissing my shoulders, he moaned out, "You are magnificent," he continued to stare at me as though I hung the stars in the sky.

I shook off my nausea as he continued his stroking and kissing my body. "With that said and done, I want to discuss something less pleasant, my brother, Michael. I can use my voice to influence Cliff and my brothers, except for Michael. Michael has this idea that he is the second coming of Christ or something and won't communicate with me except in text. He literally has founded a new religion in Louisiana, and I can't spy on him ever since he discovered that algae. He rejects any gifts and spots all the people I send. Someone who can be daring is what I need. I have been able to infiltrate every one of my siblings' plantations to learn what they are doing." I flinched when he used the word plantation. He continued, "We don't have to talk about this right now if you aren't ready. How do you feel?" He was so kind I was a little taken aback. I decided to give that some thought.

Maybe I can use this to gather more intel on him. "I'm fine, and what algae?" He gave me a blank look, so I dropped that question and continued. I'm going to need everything you have on his set-up down there.

"Well, another confession," he said while shifting me closer as though I was going to run off. "Both Cliff and I wanted Maryland, so we had a contest. A few years ago, the winner of the state was to be determined by who won The Governor's Mansion. So, making a long story short, I found out Cliff had to raise cash. He sold this drug formula to some dealers. I had the formula changed, intending to make it not provide the intended high. I figured he wouldn't get the cash to back his candidate and I would win. Instead, it caused the sterility in the black race. I have been trying to make up for that mistake for years now with my canine DNA mating programs. I try to fix my mistakes and learn from them." He smiled, obviously proud of himself. I looked at him in horror, saying, "Are you saying you and your cousin created the Drug O? He gave a self-deprecating smile, "Yeah, but it was an accident that I am fixing." I thought it was best to change the subject before I exploded in my pinned-up fury on him. Through gritted teeth, I said, "Tell me what you know about Michael's operation." He said, "Sure, I will provide you with a dossier." Great, I exclaimed. "This may be interesting. Can you get a map of the area, especially the residence? If you put them on the desk, I will study them there." He seemed pleased. "Wow, I didn't think you would be so helpful. Why are you? He asked suspiciously."

I rubbed my hand through his soft, shiny hair and smiled. My purpose was to see if he hid something there he may have used to block the gas. Next, I will start down his body for unusual moles or something that I could find. He, however, liked my stroking him and began softly kissing me. I responded the way he wanted. I soon found him shifting me to the sofa from his lap and he was lying on top of me, still kissing. It isn't hard to respond to him. Thanks to his drugs, my body wants him. There is something to that, his being my mate thing. I keep having to remind myself that, thanks to him, I no longer have a husband. Then he pulled away, and I studied every movement of his. He turned his back on me for a moment. Then, he turned back and said, "I seem to always want you, but I don't want to put any more stress on you now. You need to rest and eat soon. I took this opportunity and asked, "How long have I been here with you?" He smiled. "You are so beautiful and brilliant. I just can't give you all the secrets yet." The hissing sound started and no more consciousness for me.

Ricky's hard chest was where I woke up in the same position. My stomach growled at the smell of cooked food, so it was time for my next meal. Looking out the window, I could tell more than a few hours have passed. I lifted my head to turn to look at Ricky M., and he was grinning like The Cat that swallowed the canary. I grinned as well, "What?" I laughed. His face was so funny. His large, round, deep blue eyes, long snout-like nose and thin lips pursed into an upward tilt. He could barely contain his news. He pulled both of us up so that we were standing, and he began talking like he was holding back the best part. "Well, after the crisis with the decline of the American population over the past few years, my family has tried to find solutions. Our "territories." He put emphasis on not saying plantations. "We as a people won't survive if we don't have growth. Well, Cliff uses insemination to encourage women to carry children. I agree that if we help women who can't become pregnant normally. That's why I have a program using canine DNA. It works for most except me until now. He jumped up, pulled me with him, and spun me around in his arms. We are pregnant! You will see I will take such good care of you and our children. He kissed me all over my face. "You have given me my dream, I will never let you go." Not knowing what to say, I hesitated. After all, I want to be a mother, but with him? He released me and pulled out a chair for me to sit, and I sat, stunned. He sat in the chair adjacent, still grinning. "You are so beautiful. Eat. You need your strength, especially take your prenatal vitamins. My eyes drifted down to my plate. I sat there looking at my meal, and the grumble l in my stomach reminded me I was ravenous. I glanced up at him. I thought to myself, to think he almost soured this meal with his instructions. Haven't I been taking his vitamins all this time? I'm no child!

However, I said nothing, satisfying my hunger was more important. After all, without him, I would be locked in here with no food, so I just forced a grin and examined my plate. It was a tossed salad with grilled chicken chunks, tomatoes, cucumbers, and spinach, all with a vinegar-based dressing on the side. My mouth watered, the food looked delicious, and I dug in. To think I have rarely been this hungry, I asked if I could have some more. Ricky put a quizzical look on his face and pushed his uneaten plate to me. I didn't hesitate and ate his meal as well. I didn't speak until I finished the last morsel. I just put the food away, it took effort not to lick my fingers. Can you please leave me snacks? Ricky just kept that look on his face like he was watching a three-headed fish or something. I ignored his look but wondered why I was so hungry.

Pushing my plate away, I figured it was time to get down to business. I put the pregnancy away in the back of my head to think about later. We left the plates and the few remains of the meal there and moved to the sofa. It was time to pretend like I care about Ricky's problems. Together, we worked on Ricky's dilemma with Michael. I figured working on this will give me some clues on how to escape him. My first words to Ricky were, "So, did you get the dossier so I could help you with Michael? I'm bored here, and I would like a project." The change in direction of the conversation took him a little by surprise, but he went with it. "Yes, I put the information on the desk. We can go over it today." I smiled.

Now I have to give him something so he thinks I am happy. "Well, working on this will help me process things like my pregnancy." He perked up. I could see he was flying high while my stomach began churning in uncertainty. What do I do now? With our meal over and is now sitting on the sofa, he told me to rest. The hissing noise behind the sofa somewhere began, and I drifted off again. I am sure after his use of gas and the room cleared, we would begin working. The sun's position was something I looked at. It had moved a little, but now there were computer monitors on the desk, equipped with holographic projectors. I sat up from my normal position on his chest. I kissed his lips and ran my hands through his hair, down the nape of his neck. I found a lump that I assumed was a mole, which I now think I had better get a closer look at. I adjusted myself so that I could sit face-to-face on his lap. With the both of us naked, I could feel that move creating an erection. I should have thought of that first. I need to examine his body to discover how he can remain awake. He ran his hand through the few inches of growth in my hair. I started kissing his neck and shoulders, meanwhile looking at every lump, bump and groove on him. It looked so real to me. I thought about biting at him but dismissed it. I figured he would grow suspicious of my sudden amorous desire for him. Before I could think of a way out of this position, he was inserting himself inside me, and I just had to go with it. It wasn't unpleasant, and he held me while we again waited for my body to release him.

Once we cleaned up, we moved to the desk and began developing a plan for what to do with Michael. I began looking through the research on Michael's properties and his followers. When the light from the window hit Ricky's hair just right, I again noticed the shine. I wonder if there is something in his hair that he uses so he is not susceptible to the gas. I got to thinking about what does he do before I sleep. He usually turns his back from me, runs his hands through his hair and that is it. I have been in his hair and found nothing. I looked at the holographic screen while he was pointing at a group of poorly dressed people standing around a man that is obviously his brother. The resemblance is to Ricky M was uncanny. The man, presumably Michael, was dressed in a robe and his head was shaved in the center like a Catholic Monk.

That was weird. There is no wonder he disturbed even Ricky. Just then, I noticed Ricky's fingernails. They were slightly off-centered and raised higher off the nail than they should be. It was barely noticeable. It was there, that's it. I finally can put it together. He has either a device or a material under his nails. I would wager he uses his hair to remove the material. If it is a cream or gel, his hair would hide any residue from my sight. He could open the nails, put it on or in his nose, then rub the excess in his hair. He could do this quickly, without my notice.

Now, how to counter it is the question. "Rachel, what do you think?" He snapped his fingers in my face and I jumped. I rubbed my hands through his hair again. "Can I have some hair products now that my hair is growing out? To start, I need a comb and brush, then maybe what you are using to make your hair so soft and shiny. I put my hands to my nose and sniffed. "I added and smell so good." He didn't appear as though this bothered him and answered, "Sure, it sounds fine." I said, "Does this mean I will keep them here and comb and braid my hair when I want to, or you will take it away as you do with clothing?" He said, "It will be fine to leave the hair products in the bathroom." He smiled, lifted my chin, and kissed my lips. I smiled back and returned my attention to the holo. Now, I will see if his hair is simple products or if it is combined with something in his nails.

We continued to work through the surveillance on Michael for a couple of hours. He suggested we take a break and led me to the sofa to sit down. I asked, "Who was the man with the Leather cover

over his face that was with you when you approached me both times? His face seemed to change into something unrecognizable. His eyes darkened, a snarl came from his throat and his canines peaked out of his gums. I tried to move back away from him. He grabbed me before I could rise. Roughly, Ricky pulled me to him and held me in place. I was so scared and shaken with fear.

He looked like he was changing into a wolf. I felt my face wet with tears as he got within a hair of my nose. His breath was warm on me. I heard a whimper come out of me. He backed away suddenly. "I'm sorry," he said, and "I will not hurt you." My instincts are hard to control. You can't mention other men who are potential challengers to me. I have a hard time controlling myself, that's partly why I haven't taken you to the mansion yet. Do you understand, no other mates? I was only capable of nodding. I was truly afraid of him. He was going to eat me, I thought. I only wanted to know who that crazy man was and how can I get away from him. "I, I, I, to want to go," was all I could stutter out.

His eyes were so intense I feared he would see right through me. His mug remained in my face despite my effort to put some space between us. "You are mine, ' and his spittle flew out and landed on my face. Something switched in his face; he pulled back, and a look of remorse replaced the rage." I'm so sorry, my love. He grabbed me and wrapped me up in his arms and buried his head in my shoulder. I stiffened.

This Jeckel and Hyde routine is a bit much for me to process. "I'm sorry. I am working on controlling my rage. It is a side effect of the canine hormone boosters I take. I need you to stay with me. We need each other. Our hormonal balance is linked together for our stability. Besides, I will and could never hurt you, nor could I allow any harm to come to you. He kissed my ears and neck.

I looked down at his fingernails and could see that the index nail was askew at the base of the right hand. This was my chance. I reached up and scooped a small amount of the shiny substance that was inside. I kept it concealed on the inside of my wrist and waited. He pulled back and looked at me with tear tracks running down his cheeks. I felt little sympathy, considering I am still his prisoner. He said, "It is time for a rest while I gather myself."

I heard the hissing noise again. When he turned his back to me, I put the stolen substance underneath of my nose. Then I pretended as though I was going to sleep and started softly breathing. Judging by the drool on my chest, I think I dozed off a few times, waiting for him to do whatever he did. He must have clothes stashed somewhere because I heard bustling zippers that zip up. The room was silent after I heard footsteps moving out of the room.

After I thought he had left, I waited longer before I opened my eyes and rose from the sofa. I looked around and for the first time in I don't know how long, I was totally alone. I went to the desk and began rummaging around in the drawers but found nothing useful in them. Literally nothing at all. I could only open the computers with Ricky's optical screens, so they were useless.

I started gently knocking on the walls, trying to find which were hollow. Maybe they would open it for me. But no such luck; Ricky M must remotely operate it, guessing from the hollow sound. Searching through the bathroom cabinets, I was looking for anything useful. I, by chance, saw myself in the mirror. My hair was a tightly coiled, uncombed mess on my head that I would never have worn. My complexion had lightened in color. I guess the absence of sun or whatever he has injected me with caused this effect.

The most significant change is I have sprouted light hair on my cheeks, chin and around my eyes. That was disturbing, and I didn't see that in any of the other women. Did they shave or wax it? Was there something different about me? Was Ricky ever going to mention this to me? I sat on the restroom floor and, lifted my feet to my face and examined the rounded shape of my toes, the thickening of the nails and the sheer length of them. What is happening to me, and what will these children be?

I got up and searched the bathroom and found nothing. Looking at the sun, I used this and the best guess and assumed it's been about an hour since he has been gone. I wiped the remaining substance from my nose and returned to the sofa. My legs felt heavy just walking that short distance. Yawning before I sat, I made it to the sofa and fell asleep. I woke in the same manner as every other time. My head was resting on Ricky's chest as again. What is his purpose for positioning me in the bed on his chest every time? Is it so I could have his scent? If that is the case, he has long since achieved that, so why does he continue to do it? This time, I had a little knowledge behind me but far more questions.

Chapter 14
Childhood Traumas

When I opened my eyes, he was stroking my back. Before I even sat up, Ricky M. began talking. I think he had a hard time with this story face to face, so I remained where I was.

He began speaking, "When my brothers and I were kids, there was a lot of violence in our home. My dad took his anger out on my older brothers and they on me. I often ran off to the neighbors' yard, where they kept dog kennels, and I hid. I would sneak into the wooden dog houses to avoid the blows by whoever was after me."

Ricky pushed my body back down when I tried to sit up. So I remained there, lying on his chest. Ricky ran his hand through his hair before using it to make circles on my arm. Fixing his eyes forward, he sighed and continued. "The dogs were large and mean but would allow me in because I brought them snacks on my good days. I've always had a special connection with animals, for the most part, they were my only friends. Anyway, Michael was the worst of my brothers. He was always angry and cruel to everyone, including animals. I will spare you the details. Suffice it to say that kind of cruelty doesn't disappear in adulthood. In any case, that was where my affection for canines came."

Ricky M was deep in his memories now, and I just lay there patiently.

"Well, one day, I was hiding from Michael after Dad had given him a hard beating. He was so angry and was looking for an outlet. Michael viciously attacked all the dogs barehanded, like a crazy person. They fought back equally, and I hid in the dog house. Michael could see me behind the dogs and yelled out that he would take my protectors away.

He went after the pups first and strangled two bare-handed before the adult dogs stopped him. I came out of my hiding place and tackled him. I was no match for him, but we fought. He beat me. The dogs attacked en masse and bit him in several places. He finally stopped fighting, and the dogs did the same. There was blood everywhere. Well, he ended up in the hospital, then had multiple stitches, and later scars on his face and hands."

Ricky finally sat up and pulled me to his lap, looking me in the eyes and saying, "I'm not perfect. I want to be a better man. However, Michael is dangerous, and he has always been a threat to me in particular."

I felt compassion for this man. "Childhood can be hard, why do you still hold a grudge?" The glare he turned on me was chilling.

He grouched through clenched teeth, "That's just the tip of his cruelty. Every girl that had any interest in me he tried to steal from me. Then, if he managed to woe her away, then he would be even more cruel to her. I don't think I can fully make you understand the depth of the depravity he wreaked on these girls. He is both handsome and charismatic, or at least some people think so."

I don't know what he read on my face, but he changed the subject. "The drug that my cousin Cliff has created has incredible healing properties as well as life-extending. All of us have taken the drug, with certain agreements made between us as brothers. We don't interfere with each other's plantations, especially the families. Everyone else runs legitimate businesses that benefit the surrounding communities, including the schools and hospitals. However, Michael has used this to convince his followers that he is a prophet or a God.

The drug explains the fact his scar tissue is gone, and he demonstrates his healing to his followers. That's all I know, and I need to make sure he is not hurting anyone. This fact is combined with a successful business he has in the swamp, growing some kind of algae that is cheaper and more durable than wood. This keeps him wealthy as well. I'm telling this for your help and I want you to get to know me. To my regret, I won't be able to keep you here at my fingertips forever. You must have your freedom, and you will have it. Just please give me a little more time. In a matter of a few months, one of my most promising Bitches will give birth."

My head snapped up to look him in the eye questioningly. He stared at me for a moment, then cleared up the message. "I have altered the DNA of all my animals and there is one that is most promising. Her intelligence level is higher than all my past animals, and I'm sure her offspring will be remarkable. One will be a companion and protector for our family," With that, he kissed me on my forehead. I couldn't help my heart melt a little at the pleading look in his eyes. Yet, I still want my freedom and the choice for the other women to remain with their chosen spouses. I just couldn't come up with a response to his declarations.

Ricky would have a better chance of convincing me of his sincerity if he stopped drugging me. But since he just did it again, I figured that was a little insight into who he is, and he doesn't plan to stop. I will keep to myself. He pulled me to my feet, and we went to the desk to work again. The previous discussion is now replaced with his scheme to thwart his brother. "I want Michael to be dependent on me for something so I can keep an eye on him, and he doesn't make me a target. He doesn't accept anything from me, yet I know he is up to something. If I can find a way to gaslight him and make him want to come to me, with hat in hand."

He stopped and looked at me with pleading eyes. This I found hard to resist. Everything in me wanted to scream; he was the enemy, but little by little, he was weakening my resistance to him.

Ricky M looked back at the map on the desk and resumed, "Maybe he would ask me for a favor to fix the problem, then he will depend on me and not scheme against me. This is the reason we all agreed as teens to live in separate sections of the country.

Each slice of the country is sovereign territory, and permission has to be granted to enter. If not, then one could face penalties from the others. They can be as severe as possibly taking your children or wife."

I looked at him like if this is what it's like to have siblings, then I am truly blessed to have none. This family is past the crazy stage into outright insanity. Since obviously I couldn't go anywhere, I just sat there and listened to him numbly.

He continued, "The question is, what does he need? I have thrown women, drugs, and money, and he has turned them down. If you put fear in him, maybe he would come running to me for help. I've tried it before, and my gaslighting episode did not go so well. When I introduced a variable into Clifford's drug, O, that he was using to raise money with the drug dealers, it resulted in a cancer-causing agent in African Americans. That went worse than I intended. I just wanted to get even with Clifford for winning Maryland, our home state, as his territory. It should have been mine. We both backed different candidates for governor, and the winner determined who had the state. Well, I didn't like losing, so I spiked the drug he put on the streets. Fortunately, my family blamed him and didn't figure it was me, so that worked out. The drug combination that he perfected that extends our lives was unaltered. My gaslighting career is over, I require somebody else a lot better at it than I am. I need to get Michael wanting to help me and be on my side, and that's where you come in. I require you to do what you do best." Swallowing down my revulsion at his statements, I found a way I could take advantage of his request. So I asked, "Will I earn some freedom here as well?" His face darkened. "Like, what?" I thought about this, I need to start small in my little prison here. "I would like some hair products, to have some choice in meals, I want some deserts and snacks, and some more dresses."

He relaxed, then laughed. Well, those are all reasonable. Looking back at the pictures of the robbed Michael, I and said, "Maybe some

books on the Catholic religion. I don't even know Michael, but what
I do need is pictures, lots and lots of pictures. I need to see his home
inside out, his business inside and of out, and all the vendors and the
people that he works with. Ricky's mood had lightened considerably.

He said, "I'm going to have a lot of trouble getting to the inside
because he has fortified everything against me. We have done this
dance before, he and I, so that I will get you the outside pictures.
Look, we all have special healing properties because of the drugs
we are taking. Well, the scar tissue Michael had on his face from
the dog attack from our childhood has vanished." He uses this as
an example of his divinity. He has worshipers and everything. It's
disgusting and I think it should end. My brothers disagree and say
we all agreed to stay out of each other's territories and to leave how
he runs it up to him. It's obvious you don't believe me, and I suspect
there are unscrupulous people working for me, but I don't want to be
worshiped, feared, or hated. I want to help those who can't conceive
find their proper mate and want to raise a family with you. I know
you need freedom. You will have it. Just give me a little more time
to get my emotions under control. Ok, what else do we need to help
with getting to Michael? I gave it a lot of thought, "Truly, if I could
get inside that house. Barring that and all things considered, let me
have time to digest what you have and what I have asked for. Less
sleep time would help." I looked up at him. He smiled, "You say that
now, in a few months, you will sing a different tune." He rubbed my
flat belly. Then, he kissed my lips.

Some time went by. I have no way to tell. Ricky M said my
sleep time was less, but how could I know? I still woke up with my
head resting on his chest every time. He told me it was a scent of
mates thing. He required my scent as much as I needed his scent.
It's hard for me to come to terms with the fact he is my captor,
yet I require his touch, voice, and scent. I would understand better
when we were apart. I spent my days reading a variety of books

on Catholicism. The pictures looked like he based his religion on Catholic Monks, judging by his haircut, clothing, and the jewelry he was wearing. I looked through the photos and his background and began coming up with ideas. One moment, I felt fine, over the desk; the next, the world spin and nauseous. Ricky M's face scrunched up in confusement, it was downright comical the way he looked at me. He said, "You looked a little green." Then I felt my stomach do a flip. I ran to the bathroom and barely got to the toilet before my last meal made a reappearance. The vomit came again, and this time, Ricky was at my side. I turned and looked at him. His look was both shock and wonder. I shouted, "Can you get me something for my nausea?" He mumbled, "I don't think it is safe." I just gave him a dirty look as I felt the queasy feeling again. Just as I regained my feet to face him, vomit rose into my mouth, and it spilled onto his chest. Fear momentarily gripped me. I knew it wasn't intentional, but what did he think? He looked at the brown, chunky liquid rolling down his muscled chest and mumbled, "I'll see what I can do." Returning to my porcelain bowel, I dry heaved a couple more times. My stomach seemed to be finally done, and I brushed my teeth. I looked down, and I noticed my baby bump for the first time. Ricky M's eyes landed there at the same time. Hands snaked out before I could react, and he then rubbed my bump. The tears in his eyes touched my heart as he said, "I promise to take such good care of all of you." He pulled me to him and held me. Time went by, I don't know, probably weeks or maybe months and every day was pretty much the same. I just exercised, gave suggestions on infiltration, as received reports on successes and failures. He insisted on sex on a regular basis. I had little say so over my own life, and it was getting to me. Ricky M. and I spent much of the day doing what he wanted, sex, food, and working on a strategy to infiltrate his brother's territory. One such day, I asked for a large paper map to study Michael's property, some things are better on paper. He used several of my suggestions, like going with a witch theme or haunting. Since he lives in Louisiana, I thought it was appropriate. If he thinks he is being hexed or cursed to soften him up.

After about an hour, everything hurt. My feet and hands looked swollen, and my back hurt. I told Ricky I needed to sit down for a moment. He looked a little surprised but made no move to stop or accompany me. He continued, looking at the notes I had made. I picked up my comb and brush and started to put my rapidly growing hair, now about four inches, into braids or twists. My fingers wouldn't cooperate with the intricate braiding and I stopped. I decided to shut my eyes for just a moment. I have not slept naturally since I have been here, but today, I apparently did. I dreamed I was a giant cat running through a valley. There was soft grass between my toes, sunlight on my face, and a sense of pure joy in my heart. The leather-faced man jumped out from behind a tree and hit me in the face again.

This time, I struck back with my long teeth and, bit his hand and held on. He screamed, I felt the warm blood stream down my throat. He punched me in the face with the other hand, but I held on. I snarled out loudly as he screamed, "Let go, Rachel, please. I don't want to hurt you, let go." He finally forced me to let go with one of his strikes. The room changed, and I was trapped in a white room and a voice was shouting something at me I couldn't understand. I was at the walls and was banging on them to let me out. Now I'm a child again, trapped in the vent of a building alone.

I cried and yelled out, "Mommy and Daddy, come get me, I'm trapped." I banged on the walls with my hands, I scratched and kicked and no one came. Someone grabbed me around my waist and held my hands down. I kicked and screamed to get free. I tried to bite, but there was nothing to latch on to. I was being dragged backward. Someone was trying to kill me. Then I was being drowned. I could hear a male voice, "Wake up, Rachel! You are safe! Oh God, please wake up. I love you, I need you, please come back to me." I was suddenly aware the dream world had faded out. Strong arms held me as water poured over my body, and realization hit me. I was in the shower with Ricky M. The haze cleared as I looked at him and his face changed into that snarling beast.

Then, it remade itself into the man I had been with for the past weeks, days, months, I didn't know. I looked at myself; my black nails were jagged and broken, my hands and feet looked swollen, and there was blood, mine or Ricky's, running down my swollen abdomen. That's right, I'm pregnant, something I still haven't dealt with. Turning back to Ricky M., there were numerous scratches on his face and neck. I looked at his hands and saw the deep tooth punctures that were still bleeding. Not just one, but several bites. He released me to allow me to step away from him to see the extent of the damage. I had inflicted multiple deep lacerations on his chest and torso. Some downright puzzled me about how I could have done it.

However, it was open wounds still bleeding. I looked out of the bathroom and saw the pool of blood from the sofa, and splashed around till we arrived here in the bathroom. I didn't know if I should apologize or not. I opened my mouth to say something. He cut me off with, "Rachel, you have a deep childhood trauma that you probably aren't aware of. This is my fault for keeping you captive for so long, and I am sorry I triggered this. He pulled me to him and hugged me, "Please forgive me. I was ready weeks ago for us to move, but something scared me and, it's time, you knew what. Let's get cleaned up, and don't worry about these minor cuts.

The modifications to my body have healing properties. You won't even see them in a few days. We got cleaned up, he even pulled a dress out from some unit that melted back into the wall after revealing the contents of other clothing. I like the dress and smiled when I put it on. He held me close and said, "The suggestions you gave to make an impact on my brother over the past few weeks have made a difference. However, not the difference I wanted. Instead of him calling me and asking for help or suggestions, he sent me a warning." Now he had my complete attention. Ricky M very seldom used technology in my presence, except for when we worked on projects with Michael. He called his AI and projected a hologram for me. He continued, saying, "Michael sent me this. The display showed an opened box with of six dead black-furred puppies. A highlighted text was in the second picture, stating the following:

Abominations created betwixt thou loins
shall not be permitted to take a breath within
the space of God's Great Earth. Your violations
Of God's Law shall be smitten by the Warrior of God.

I read and reread this, feeling shock and disbelief. Is he threatening our children? Am I carrying puppies? How does he know about me?" The signs of stress in Ricky's body visibly kicked up a notch. He inhaled and breathed out slowly and began. "First, you have a normal, healthy pregnancy. Next, I am quite sure he has spies in my organization, just as I have planted inside my camp, although none of mine get very far. Therefore, that is how he knows about you, despite my best efforts. This is another reason why I haven't taken you to the mansion yet, frankly, I'm afraid. I don't know if I can protect you as well. I know you need your freedom, and it is taking a toll on your psyche. This is my fault. I promise I will fix this. You are unique, I'm still not sure if you know how much. The DNA compound I introduced has enhanced your body more than any other I have seen. I wish I could find your parents and run tests because I think you were part of triplets. One or both have been absorbed by your body, this is rare in itself, but a combination of external factors has changed you even more.

Your DNA strands have been modified, probably yours was not a natural conception." Suddenly I felt as though the oxygen had been sucked from the room, and I bent over to struggle for breath. The excitement in Ricky's voice stalled while he tried to think of what to do. Moments later, I regained my composure, straightening, I motioned with my hands he could continue.

Ricky M. picked up where he left off, "I am concerned about your pheromones. They are more potent than any I have seen before. You are going into what is similar to what some animals go through, like 'Heat.' Except instead of driving the urge to mate, yours are driving the urge to protect you. Simply put, other unmated men will find it difficult to resist the urge to protect and own you. These emotions will become overwhelming for these men and I have no idea how it may manifest. With myself, I not only want to mate and protect, I need your scent often. I am working on a counterdrug for you and me. The counterdrug I have been injecting in my body will suppress the pheromones you are putting out so that I may function normally in society, just as long as we are in regular physical contact." Surprise in my voice, I asked, "For you, "Why? Was I a designer baby, created in a lab dish and why?" He laughed and grabbed my hand, "I am your mate, where you go, I go. From what I've learned about your birth parents, they designed the three of you with specific criminal activities in mind. I have no idea if any of your siblings even lived, there is no record of other births." Giving me a pity look, he replied, "With your pheromone enhancements, I can't have others driving you crazy with their needs. Your effect on other men will be intense and increase with the rise and fall of your hormones. After all, I am your mate, and I am still trying to control my jealousy." He kissed me on my lips and said, "Please be a little more patient with me while I fix this." I know you want to be included in the decisions, and you will be soon. The hissing started and soon. My last thought before I was asleep was if he would stop putting me into a drugged sleep, it would be a first step of trust.

Chapter 15
Year 2030—What the claws!

An unknown time later, when I woke, laying on his chest, but was irritable. All my extremities throbbed, my feet, toes, hands, fingers, and even my ears. The light in the room further irritated me, giving me a headache. I wanted out of this place and Ricky to pay for trapping me here. I don't know why; maybe stress, or hormones, or captivity. As soon as I got up, I started complaining, trying to put Ricky in as much pain as I felt. "Ricky, why can't you let me have clothes here to keep? Naked all the time, I'm more like an animal in a cage, and I want to feel like a woman. I am still a woman, aren't I? I want to feel more than just your mate, whatever that means. Staying here all the time is suffocating me." I continued by screaming at the top of my lungs got no response. Tears were my next emotion, so I collapsed on the floor and just cried.

Squatting down next to me, he kissed my lips and said, "You have a purpose. I've given you a new, much more beneficial one. You are my queen, the woman to lead by my side."

I decided I had nothing to lose, so I continued to press. Besides, I wanted to see what would happen if I pushed. Would he hurt me? Possibly, but between my hormones and my aching extremities, I wanted to needle him.

"When will I be free to walk around again? To smell flowers and see the sun, feel the grass under my feet, run with the sun on my face?" I looked at him with all the longing I could put into my face.

He looked at me like these are things he never considered. His big declarations made early on meant nothing. I have returned to feeling like a bug he put under a glass and never considered the freedom he was depriving me of. He drew his eyebrows together and

185

said, "Someone may hurt you out there, as people can touch you?" He ran his hand down my hips slowly with reverence.

This crazy man believes he is saving me. I got right into his face and screamed, "A gilded cage is still a cage. I want out! Let me go, and I will take my chances with Michael, other men, anyone. I will fight to protect myself and our baby!"

He stroked my hip with his now-healed hand. That was of no consequence to me. I was on a roll. Contemplating my next move as we stood toe to toe. What I didn't know was he would reach out to touch or rub my abdomen. A growl came out of my chest that didn't seem human. It was pure instinct born of the frustration of captivity. I struck out with my mouth and a bit hard on his arm. The blood rushed into my mouth, down my throat as my canines' lockdown. This time I liked it.

Someone was screaming, only making me hold tighter until he punched me in the side of my face with his free hand. He hit me. I knew it was probably instinctive, but that didn't matter, and my full rage kicked in. We looked at each other. I released him and screamed, "Let me be free now!"

His face changed into that same look he had when I'd made him angry before. This time, I wasn't afraid. I still don't know what overcame me. After all, his look was terrifying and there was no one to rescue me. His eyes were so small, there was no white, just all-black pupils. His canines peeked out of his gums, his forehead scrunched up, and his hair seemed to stand on end. Words in growls came out, "No, you would leave me. I can't let you go." His arm dripped blood, but he ignored it. He lunged for me, attempting to wrap his arms around my abdomen.

Ricky M yelled back, "You belong to me!" His arm came close to my mouth again, and I snapped out and sunk my teeth into his flesh again while staring into his fearful eyes. I tore a chunk of skin from his forearm and swallowed it.

My face ached when he hit me while he was trying to get me to release my hold on him. The thought of that released more rage unlike any I'd ever felt before. Screaming out with the pain and rage, something remarkable happened. I'm not sure how it happened, instinct took over. I swiped with my hand, and I reached for his throat. It opened a four-clawed wound that sprouted a funnel of blood. I swiped again and landed a second blow on the left side of his face. Opening a large flap of flesh on his jaw, where I could see for a moment his teeth. I looked down at my extremities, and there were black, sharp claws retracting back into my puffy fingers. There was no time to process as I looked up to Ricky M's eyes rolled back in his head as he fell straight back on the floor.

Running into the bathroom, I retrieved a towel and wrapped it around his neck to slow the bleeding. I didn't want to hurt him. Now, what is he going to do to me? I put pressure on it. His eyes were closed. Fear and instinct commanded my decisions. As delicately as I could, I opened his eyes and took the contacts out, then placed them in my eyes. Just like I thought, they were his connection to his AI. I found the door, opened it, and then called emergency services to come to the location where I dropped a pin. I pulled up a schematic of the building to find an exit. He will probably kill me, I thought. Just then, I felt the baby move, and panic seized me.

My thoughts went back to my days in foster care, when I believed I was surrounded by enemies, and instinct took over. I need to disappear. I ran past the desks, people, guards, and everyone I encountered. There was no time to care, just fear, and the adrenaline kept my feet moving. As I moved past, I heard the clicking of my toes on the floor. I was naked but free. Nobody was going to stop or cage me. I was out, and I was on the run, maybe for murder. I ran right out of the office doors into the lobby.

When I approached the last guard station, I finally had burned off much initial burst of adrenalin. I slowed to a walk, and both guards were looking at me with mouths wide open and eyes bugging out.

I turned to the first one, a tall but portly guy, and commanded, "Give me your shirt." He took off his jacket and began unbuttoning his shirt without taking his eyes off of me.

Well, I still got it, I thought. "I turned to the other one. Give me your key fob and point out the company car you drive." He pointed out a mid-size car.

I asked the portly one, "Can you disable the tracking device?"

He answered, "No, only Ricky M can disable them."

Ok, I thought, then wait a moment. I have his contacts. I put on the guard's shirt, then his belt to make it a dress. Through the contacts, I searched for Ricky's files. I could delay the report, but to disable the car, the file's encryption will take too long for now. I told the men not to report to anyone they had seen me and to return to work as they were before I came. They turned their back to do just that.

I got in the car and was off, my old house is where I went first. After retrieving my to-go bag, I sent Mrs. Miller a fax to tell he caught me, but I escaped. The plan has failed, and I will make my way to Maryland to meet her. Then I changed into a pair of old torn jeans, a blue sweater, tennis shoes, and a jacket, so blending in would be easy. I couldn't keep the stolen car or clothes long, so I drove it to a parking lot to ditch it. My plan was to travel on foot for a while until I found a vehicle that was in a more secluded area. Then I would steal it for travel. I was still in the lot of dumping the clothes when I spotted some of Ricky M's guards getting out of an SUV, presumably to look for me. *They must have already tracked that car. How else did they find me so fast*, I thought. If I get in any car now and drive, they will surely spot me. Ok, I thought, *I would wager Ricky M did something to them to overcome my influence, so they would only listen to him and not me anymore. I would also guess they can smell me, and they won't risk true harm to me because I am carrying his children. So, what do I do with this information? My scent needs to be masked. I looked for a gas-powered truck or SUV.*

After locating a late-model Nissan, I rolled under it. Next, I smudged some engine debris on my face and exposed skin to disguise my scent. Scooting out from under, careful of my abdomen, I searched for the location of the men. They were doing a car-by-car search, looking inside about a quarter mile from me. That was way too close. I started looking for a dumpster or trash receptacle to hide and find nothing. From the direction of the sun, I heard a familiar voice calling my name. *Impossible*, I thought. He couldn't be up and talking so soon. I looked up at a drone a few feet over the guards. One moment, there was the drone, the next, Ricky's face was overlaid.

Ricky M's voice stated: "Come back, Rachel, it's ok. My men won't hurt you or my children. I know you're scared and didn't mean to hurt me. I understand your hormones are driving you. We can talk about this. Come home to me where it is safe, and I will take care of you again."

Still staring at the sphere in the sky, I blinked several times to make sure I wasn't hallucinating. It was true, Ricky M's image was overlapping the drone, and he was seemingly injury-free. That was curious. However, just like everything else, there was no time to process. Nothing for me has changed. I have no ill will for Ricky now that I have gotten to know him. He is highly misguided and worth some sympathy, but no way am I ever willingly going back there. I don't want to be caged, even though I believe on some level physically I already am. Just the sight of him made my body want to go to him, but I still have my own mind and that was not happening. It suddenly dawned on me: How could I be so stupid? The damned contacts. He tracked me through them, and that's why I saw his face over the drone. Of course, he can manipulate images with them, they are his. I plucked them from my eyes and tossed them on the ground before smearing them in with the heel of my shoe.

Glancing out from around a parked Tesla, I can only see one of the searching men now. He was looking inside the cars. Where did the other one go? A scent hit me as the hair on the back of the back of my neck stood on end. The urge to leave was overwhelming. My feet began moving before my brain caught up. My instincts screamed it's time to go. I started backing away from the man I could see. My back hit something solid. It was the missing guard. He wrapped his arms around me, one around my chest and the other around my waist, just under my abdomen. I struggled. He lifted me totally off the ground as I kicked, snarled, and I bit into him.

I could hear the voice of Ricky M saying, "No, don't hurt my queen, don't hurt my young, she will fight back hard."

Too late. The guard wrapped his arms around me in a vice grip, one around my breast and the other had slipped up to around my abdomen. Rational thought left my brain at the thought of him hurting my baby.

An uncharacteristic voice came out of me again as the growl emanated from my chest.

Ricky yelled frantically, "No, not around her belly! Let her go now. Instinct will kick in. She's going to fight to protect her young!"

Anger hit its boiling point, this time, I felt my claws come out. My once pinned hands began from his legs and moved upward. My claws broke through the pants to split the skin. I followed his legs up as I reached out to dig through flesh and sinew. Once the pain registered, his arms released me. My claws were like daggers now as I ripped them up the side of his face. Blood gushed out, and his scream was muffled by the flaps of torn flesh as he pushed me away from him. The other man came rushing out, pulling a weapon to point at me.

Ricky growled out, "No, weapons, if you shoot her, you die next."
I turned around and braced for an attack from the man. The man
took a look at his partner, who had slumped to the ground in a pool
of blood. Wisely, he returned the gun to its holster and approached
me, hand up in surrender. I would kill him if I had too, he will not
take me back. With hands raised and mouth gaping open, he was
just standing still, waiting for me to make a move. His inaction was
the only thing that was keeping him alive. With my claws extended,
kicking off my shoes extended the claws on my feet, I turned and ran.
Moving over the ground so fast, I felt nothing. I ran until I found a
patch of woods to enter. Putting distance between myself and them.
Mindlessly, I ran until all the adrenaline drained out of my system,
and finally, I was exhausted. Coming back to my senses, it surprised
me by the distance I covered. The sun has set now. I didn't have any
idea where I was, but I was free. Needing to find shelter, I looked
around, trying to find a house with a basement and low security that
I could creep into. It wasn't long before I spotted one climbed into
the window. The room was gloomy, but my vision had improved over
the past months. I couldn't see color, but I could make out shapes.
Feeling around for something soft to lie on were my only thoughts. I
found what felt like a sofa, and I was spent. I curled up and fell asleep.
The sound of footsteps and voices upstairs woke me a time later.
Straining as much as I could, I couldn't quite make them out. As
quietly as possible, I got up. I started trying to locate the window that
I entered through, but now there was almost no light. I didn't know
what to do. Worse yet, I heard what sounded like a basement door
open. A moment later, I clearly heard a woman's voice say, "Search
the basement for her." They are looking for me, now what? I put my
hands out and tried to find the window by memory, but the sound of
the footsteps coming down was in that direction, so I started backing
up. I turned back to see where I was going, and for a moment, I
thought I saw a large shadow move, but I didn't smell anyone. Now I

am freaking myself out. No, someone was here and they are moving. I started backing up with every step the intruder took forward. Hands gripped my mouth, and the other restrained my hands and pulled me back.

A man's voice whispered in my ear, "Don't panic, I'm here to help." Normally, I would have still panicked, but instinctively, I felt this man was a safer bet. I nodded my head and relaxed against his body. He released my mouth and pulled me into the deep recess of a shadow with him. I barely breathed as a flashlight swayed back and forth in a search pattern that lasted for hours or minutes. It was so long and I was so scared. It was one thing to fight or scheme when scared, but to wait is the worst. Finally, satisfied, the basement was empty, and the footsteps retreated upstairs. The search party departed the house a short time later. I stepped away from the man who protected me. He spoke again, "Jack, my family and I have been trying to rescue you for months. That crazy man had you pinned up tight. I am good, but that paranoid maniac changed his system so often that I couldn't break it. John, Adam and I came to retrieve you. We took turns over the weeks waiting for an opportunity to bring you to safety. Mrs. Miller sent me. You had other women concerned for your welfare that I have been in contact with. The women told me you would believe me if I told you their names: Strawberry Crêpes, Tortellini, and Chocolate Beignet." He stopped talking long enough to studying me, maybe he thought the names were incorrect. We kept drones up looking out and when a naked woman went running through the lot of the corporation, I started following you. You lost me several times, but I guessed when I caught up with you in the woods, you would look for a basement to break into. So I waited. You were fine to sleep until they came looking for you. Before I could wake you, you woke up. I didn't want you to claw me like you did that guard. I thought I'd wait until you were in trouble and save you.

Out came the most disarming smile I have ever seen. I think I'm going to like this guy.

He said, "Hey, how did you know I wasn't going to hurt you?" I thought about this and answered, "You smell familiar to me, although I don't think I have ever met you. Are we related somehow? I don't know any of my family. I know you smell like me, though."

He laughed a little and said, "Well, that may be good for my health, Jack Scissorhands." He chuckled, "My name is Ralph. Mrs. Miller is a good woman. She lived in Maryland when I was a kid and cared for me when my parents abandoned me. I owe her and do whatever she asks." He dusted himself off, showing share time was over. "Let me go outside first to make sure things are clear, then are you well enough to follow? Did Ricky M hurt you, other than the obvious?" He stared momentarily at my slightly protruding abdomen.

I said, "No, I can travel, I am carrying his young and he will kill you or anyone else to get us back."

Ralph pulled out a gun from his holster and said, "There is a long waiting list of people trying to take me out."

He took a couple of steps forward, stopped and, turned and asked, "By any chance, are you planning on nursing your children?"

I was not expecting that question, stuttering, "I haven't thought about it." He turned back around without another word and went up the stairs. I thought, what a bizarre question. He returned a short time later. We jogged out to his car, which was parked a couple of miles away.

We were off, and I was looking at the grass again and breathing fresh air. No matter what happens five minutes from now, I am content now. I looked at the claws on my hands, and they had retracted into my puffy fingers and the ones on my feet. Ok, that, I guess, is my new reality.

We drove for about thirty minutes. The breeze on my face and the sound of the car's engine were hypnotic. This is the first time I have been relaxed in months, and I spent most of that dozing. Ralph was quiet, with his eyes forward and a blank expression on his face, before he pulled off at a convenience store. Another car was waiting in the parking lot. It had a key fob in an envelope under the driver's seat. Turning to look at him, questioning but saying nothing as we walked inside the convenience store long enough for me to relieve my bladder. When I came out feeling lighter after relieving myself, Ralph had picked up some food he apparently ordered in advance and then got into another car. My first thought was, how did he make the order without me hearing anything? Next, it was, he could have asked me what I liked. The burgers and fries smelled so good that I just accepted mine and dug in. I found it was delicious, but I was still hungry. "Do you have anything else to eat?" He hadn't even touched his burger, only a few fries. He tossed me the bag without turning his head. I didn't give it a second thought and consumed that as well. Wow, that hit the spot. I sat back on my seat and rubbed my slightly protruding belly.

Ralph reached behind him, grabbing a large box. Just as I got my seatbelt on, he tossed the box into my lap, barely missing my almost empty food bag.

"Well, are you comfortable flying by chopper to Clifford Matthews in Maryland? We can't take any to chance of being tracked too quickly. We are quite certain you have an internal bug." He glanced down at the box while he spoke, then up to eye him curiously. "Those are some clothes Mrs. Miller ordered for you so you look decent." I had been naked long enough. I stopped thinking about what I was wearing, really, except for nagging Ricky M. None of the rest had occurred to me. The look on my face betrayed my feelings because he continued.

"Think about it, Jack, you really think that Ricky would not have put trackers inside your body somewhere.? The man is obsessed with you, and I use the term man loosely. We must keep moving until we are out of his territory."

I needed to calm my nerves with a change in conversation. I asked him to tell me about his life as I changed. He sensed that is what I needed and explained he shared two children with John and Marilyn now. The bra and panties were lying on top of the box. Squealing in delight, I was so happy to see these again. Ralph gave me a look like he was questioning my sanity, but I ignored him. With delight, I jerked off my shirt with no regard for the man driving and began working on the bra.

Ralph stopped in mid-sentence to explain that they were expecting triplets soon, which they also shared with Adam. Looking at my bare breasts, he shrugged his shoulders, then returned his eyes to the wheel and continued his dialogue. He had to explain how that worked. It is the 21st century and all kinds of things are possible. He talked proudly about his son, JR and how much he loved him. Only slightly offended, I knew my breasts were not impressive. He told me his childhood was only bearable because of his grandmother and Marilyn's family.

I continued to dress and even unintentionally put my ass in his face while trying to maneuver around my clothes.

He shoved it aside so his view of the road was unobstructed and continued talking. After that, I felt I needed to share and told him my parents left me in a jewelry store while committing a heist. Social Services passed me around in foster care until I aged out.

He was somber in his memories, Ralph added, "My parents were con artists, that would have been my fate if grandmother hadn't interfered. Later, Mr. and Mrs. Chane, as well as the neighborhood, took care of me until I could support myself." I noticed we were pulling up to a field that had a small helicopter waiting in the middle that was starting up. I looked at the craft, then looked at Ralph. He had his face straight ahead but must have sensed my distress. "Don't be afraid, believe me, it's okay. We will further discuss this in the chopper." He added a reassuring smile. We boarded the craft and once settled, I relaxed. Ralph handed me an AI and holographic imager. I put them in place on my face and wrist so we could talk by just moving our lips despite the sound of the rotors. Ralph adjusted himself and got Mrs. Miller on the other end of the device. She looked to be in a bedroom with white walls. "Now that we are all on, we all need to tell everything we know," Ralph said.

I saw Mrs. Miller for the first time in several months, and I almost broke out in tears just seeing a familiar face. I wish I could hug her, and I am not a touchy, feely person, but my emotions were on edge. "It is so nice to see you, Rachel Lynn. I was worried sick about you. The tears in her eyes started, and then mine began to flow. Ralph told me you were alive months ago, but he couldn't reach you. I don't want to gush on, so I will get down to business. Clifford Matthews has custody of your and Shane's son, Thomas. His birth mother, Penelope, gave birth to him using the fertilized eggs, then died shortly after. Clifford has had nannies carrying for him since. There is more. The elderly woman's eyes darkened, and I knew this wasn't going to be good. She cleared her throat first. Your genetic material has been shipped all over the country for the past five years." She paused to wait for my reaction.

Moments later, my brain caught up to what she was implying. "Wait, What? How could my eggs have been distributed for the past five years? Shane only signed away my material a few years ago."

A frown crossed her lined face. "You've met Sandy? Well, she and her husband have been the administrator of IVF clinics for the past decade. In the past five years, several of their clients have signed their material back over to the company and others have just gone missing. I suspect they are selling this material to the highest bidders.

Shane is not likely the first or last man conned. I'm sorry dear, I don't have anything else good to tell you. Your child living with Clifford Matthews is the only live birth I could locate. Although this is probably of little consequence, I don't think Ricky M was aware of the business that Sandy and her husband were running. They were sending out trans-speciecs individuals to blackmail spouses all over the country into signing the genetic material back over to them. Ricky M's name wasn't on any paperwork except for the material that went to his brothers and Aunt Penelope." The elderly woman sighed and her eyes showed exhaustion as well as relief. She spoke again, "OK, Ralph will fill you in on all of what Cliff is capable of, so be aware. You must make him believe you can offer him something to make it worth his while."

Ralph spoke up and told me the long story of his interactions with Cliff.

When it was my time to share, I gave them everything from the time I met Shane. Mrs. Millers chimed in with questions for clarity here and there before we began discussing strategy. All the mistakes, cowardice, and my arrogance that led to the death of my husband. I understand now that I want to be a better person for my children, including Thomas. With limited time, there was no one left for me to ask forgiveness to, so I put my shortcomings to the back of my mind. The three of us came up with several ideas on how to protect me and allow me to have a relationship with my son. We came back around to the same thing. We must convince Cliff Matthews, Ricky M's cousin, to protect me from Ricky and Michael's war. Ralph and his family (John, Adam, and Marilyn) have a relationship with Cliff and will look in on me to make sure no harm comes to me. Apparently, Cliff has a drug that all the Matthew brothers must take annually to extend their lives, so that lends credence to what Ricky was saying. We are on our way to the mansion now. Ralph wants me to meet and work with his partner Marilyn, but she is carrying triplets and recently lost her mother. Ralph asked me not to speak to her until after the children were born. He wants her stress levels kept low. I will, however, meet the other partners, Adam and John, at the mansion as well.

Ralph thrust a tablet into my hands. "Order a few outfits. When done, I will have them delivered to Adam's house. So you will have something and somewhere to go in case things don't work out. I did so as frugally as possible. We should land in an hour."

We've arrived at the Mansion and landed on the Helios pad on the roof. Dressed, I am ready for business or war. It was time for the burning question to be answered before I was ready for the game of convincing this stranger to protect me. "Ralph, I asked, "How long was I held prisoner? His brown eyes roamed my face before answering, "Four months." My hand flew to my chest as my lungs grabbed for air. I knew more than a few weeks past, but months. We sat in silence.

The copter landed on the top of a building equipped for such landings. A woman dressed in a tailored suit was there to greet us. She introduced herself as Wren Fields and didn't offer her hand; she just instructed me and my party to follow her. The tall, brown-skinned woman had her hair in a severe bun and judging by her rigid walk, I would guess she was or was military. Her black suit was pressed to within an inch of its life, and she wore no makeup. Wren led us down several corridors that I am sure I would never find my way back through until we reached two large wooden doors. She opened the doors and ushered us in before turning on her heel, shutting the doors and leaving.

We walked into an opulently furnished room. Behind the desk was what I presumed to be Clifford. He was a small framed man, probably in his mid-to-late sixties. Sandy hair, brownish eyes, wearing a smarmy look on his face, like he knows something that we don't. He looks like maybe an accountant or a used car sales associate, definitely somebody I would never have trusted. He resumed the sitting position, sitting behind a large, brown oak dress desk. In the corner, now standing in front of two large overstuffed chairs, were two men. One was a black man, well-dressed and very nice-looking. He was tall, well-built in a blue suit and standing beside him was a white man equally tall, well-built and very handsome.

Before they could give introductions, Clifford spoke. "My time is short, and I want to get on with this meeting." The double doors behind me opened and Mrs. Miller entered the room with one of Cliff's men. I was glad to see her, however, despite the situation, we hugged, and she stood by the men. She was apparently familiar to them. She greeted them loud enough that now I knew who was who. Ralph also found a seat in the same area, leaving me standing alone in the center of the room.

Cliff impatiently blurted out, "My cousin is going to be very upset that you have his wife." He addressed this to Ralph. The animosity was obvious. I didn't react to the name to title being a wife, but I started speaking before anyone else. "I have something that he wants, and I'm offering it to you." Clifford looked at me up and down like I was a hooker.

"What is it I can't get other places?" he said. "This had better be good and worth me warring with my brothers," he grouched out. I already didn't like this man, but I spoke with my life on the line, "Clifford Matthew's come here and kneel before me," I ordered.

He stopped talking, and his face went blank. Without another word, he emerged from behind the desk and, walked right in front of me and stood. He got on his knees without saying a word. Next, I ordered, "Kiss my feet," and he bent over, puckered up and with a flourish, he kissed them both. I heard the seated men snicker at Cliff's actions. Then, like the fool that I sometimes am, I stood there grinning, all proud of myself and took my eyes off of Cliff. Without a word, in a single motion, Cliff stood up, pulled down his trousers, pulled out his manhood, grabbed me by the waist, turned me around, yanked down my pants and put himself inside of me. He was raping me before I gathered what was happening. Adam and Ralph went into motion and pulled him off of me and had him pinned on the floor with his junk still hanging out. He was lying there looking totally dazed. I looked at Cliff as I readjusted my clothes. Some of that chip was now off his and my shoulder. He looked at me with a disgusted look as he scrambled to his feet and readjusted his clothes. He backed away from me, never taking his eyes off me, while he returned to behind his desk.

Mrs. Miller was so excited. "This is so amazing. I remember at my house, it was something similar. Your abilities seem to be a lot stronger now. Are her sexual pheromones affecting the three of you men as well?"

I caught John trying to readjust himself. Ralph said, "I felt nothing sexual toward her." He shrugged. "Sorry, I mean, you are attractive, but your breasts and ass are just too small for me. Besides, sex with you might get me all cut up with those Scissor hands of yours." His face frowned up as he eyed my hands, which looked normal right now. Annoyed, I looked for something to throw at him but found nothing. I smiled. I actually like this guy. "You know, I really like your bluntness."

Adam and John looked at each other. Adam spoke up, "Ever since she came in the room, we both feel as though we want to her. It is difficult to resist."

Mrs. Miller said, "While the compulsion must only work on some men, but that and the sex drive is more intense. However, the level of self-control and if they are aware of it in advance, as both Adam and John were, may make a difference. Cliff was taken completely by surprise, making him more susceptible."

Cliff shook his head in agreement, "Yeah, I think I can handle myself now. I can see why my cousin wanted to keep you all to himself. He was probably afraid to let you go. You are like some kind of succubus. Did you say Ricky M can use this on me? Mrs. Miller said he has been using his voice to influence me for some time." I answered, "Yes, he can and has. However, I am stronger than he is." Cliff looked more in his element now.

He turned to speak to Adam. "I can work with this. The five-year Marriage Contract is something I agree with." I walked close to Adam and got in his face.

"Marriage? Oh hell no, am I going to marry him!" I exclaimed while pointing to Clifford. "I just met him two minutes ago." Mrs. Miller said, "Rachel Lynn, do not be so hasty and remember, you are pregnant. You need to calm down and listen to reason. You can always divorce if things go wrong. But at least a marriage will give you certain protections from Ricky and Michael. You will also gain custody of Thomas, your son. Ricky M wants to own you and the children you are caring for. The men have set up sovereign territories, and as his wife, you are protected in this territory.

Cliff added, "She's exactly correct. I know my brothers will never stop. They both want something. You have Ricky's children. How many are you having, anyway?" Bewildered, I responded, "I do not know, he never told me." Cliff hurumped, "Well, that's one thing we'll have to clear up. Meanwhile, yes, we will have to be married."

The other men in the room looked at me. Ralph said, "Don't worry, we have your back. We will all look out for you. We will not allow Cliff to put you in the cage like Ricky. Cliff's face drew together, reacting to the distaste he felt before responding, "I have no desire to put you in a cage. However, I will offer you my protection. I will have some female bodyguards watch and care for you at all times. I need your talents. They are extremely valuable to me. This will be a marriage of partnership. You will never have to be in my bed unless you want to. You can go back to or have sex with Ricky if you choose, but remain married to me. Cliff's eyes grew wide. He was receiving a message through his AI that surprised him. Cliff asked, "Do you agree to the terms?" I looked at Mrs. Miller. She nodded. Ralph nodded, then Adam, who also nodded. I said, "I agree." Cliff shouted, "We are under attack!"

The men leaped off their feet, and the doors burst open before they could react. In walked Ricky M. He wore dark blue military-style fatigues, with guns and knives strapped to him. I could now hear gunfire outside the door. I couldn't help it. My heart leaped with joy to see him again. Ricky shouted, "Everyone in the room, stay where you are! The men (Cliff, Adam, and John), except for Ralph, all froze in place. Several other men that I assumed to be Ricky's entered the room because they were dressed in fatigues similar to Ricky's. They sported earwear, guns, and knives. The canine features were dead giveaways once I got a close look at them.

Ralph seemed conflicted about whether to protect me or Mrs. Miller. That became clear as one of the men struck the old woman on the temple, and she collapsed. Ralph jumped to catch her. I leaped to her and Ricky intercepted me. He grabbed hold of my hands and pulled me into his chest. I inhaled and for a moment, I wanted to stay with him, as I recognized my mate.

He looked into my eyes and pleaded with me, "Please, don't move. I need to talk to you to explain. Cliff is my brother, but you are my queen and I love you." I kept that in the back of my head that Cliff referred to his cousin as brother as well. The sincerity I read in his eyes knocked me for a loop. I couldn't think for a moment. Now, I have had two men who truly feel they loved me. I still don't know for sure what to make of my own feelings.

Before there was time to unpack this, the movement behind Ricky M. caused me to gasp. He turned in time to see the entry of another man. This one I recognized from the pictures as Michael. Michael was wearing what I can best describe as a combat version of a robe. It still had the basic design of a robe, yet it was more flexible, with pockets containing what I assume were weapons. He shouted out like he was on some pulpit, "Thoust has created an abomination within her womb, I shall take her to cast it into the fires of hell whence it came!"

Ricky turned and said, "Everyone in the room, be as you were." I guess he realized he could not beat Michael without Cliff's help. Cliff, John and Adam all immediately joined the side facing the newcomers. Ricky was still holding my hands, and I stood at the entrance door with Michael to the left of us. Ralph was still on the floor to the right, with Mrs. Miller in his lap. Her head was actively bleeding. She appeared unconscious, and my temper was rising.

Cliff tried to gain control of the situation by announcing, "You are all on my plantation uninvited, and I want you to leave." Ricky said, "Yes, that is fine." He released one of my hands and squeezed my other tighter as he started pulling me behind him.

Cliff, Adam, and Ralph shouted, "No, not with her." Just then, a trio of leather-faced men entered. Gunshots rang out. I could only process a thin trail of smoke at first coming from the fired weapons. Turning on my heel, seemingly in slow motion, I watched first Cliff, then John, then Adam all fall. My brain caught up as I realized the man or his team had shot them. Michael dropped as well. Then there was chaos. When the gun swung toward Ralph, Ricky, with his speed, hit the man in the jaw. Ricky M took me to the floor, covering my body with his own while others shot him. Fighting broke out between the men of all parties. Masked soldiers wearing earpieces and black vests are in the room, holding smoking handguns. Ricky released me, rolled off of me and was on the ground with holes in his chest. One of the Leather-faced men grabbed me by the hand and tried to drag me out of the room. I have had enough. My claws came out as my hands gouged his arm to the wrist. He released my hold, and I kicked off my shoes. My feet claw extended, and I screamed with everything I had, "STOP, DON'T TOUCH ME!"

Their earpieces negated my orders but not my fight. Another tried to take me and I started fighting them. Ralph gained his feet and was fighting as well.

Sudden pain lit up in my head, and then the lights went out after someone got a lucky punch. I woke up to being dragged by my hands. The sunlight hit my face as we exited the house. Several sounds like skin against skin, then gunshots, and I heard the most inhuman roar ever. The hands dragging me dropped me hard on the gravel stone. Stars filled my vision, then blackness. When I regained awareness, I sat up and tried to focus. I made out a bloody man's back, running toward a waiting car that was parked on the grass of the grounds a short distance away. Turning to look to the right, on the grass about ten feet away lay Ralph, beaten and eyes closed. I crawled to him, I put my hand on his neck and found a strong pulse. I hoarsely called, "Ralph, are you okay?" He smiled through cracked and bleeding lips, "No, someone has been in a fight. But I think he will live, too." This man is a nut case, I thought. I heard moaning. I looked and saw another broken body. "Oh, my God, I screamed, Ricky." I hastened to reach him. He was bleeding from many gunshot wounds. I took off my shirt, tore it, and tried to slow the bleeding. Now, I heard the sirens approaching. He didn't open his eyes but said, "I'm sorry I didn't let you free earlier. I just couldn't lose you. Please kiss me one more time." I cried as I remembered how he covered my body with his own and took the gunshots. Looking into his face, I said, "You are my mate; I know this. I was just scared. I think I might even love you." He closed his eyes as his breathing slowed. One side of his lip was turned up in a smile. With gentle kisses, I lay beside him, with my arms wrapped around his bleeding chest, until the EMTs came and loaded Ricky and all the unconscious people before treating the injured.

The police questioned those who were standing. Most were the fighting men of different parties, and they refused to answer. After the arrests were made and the combatants were taken to various vehicles that were constantly streaming in, my adrenaline left my body. When the police got to me and asked what exactly was going on here, I couldn't think clearly enough to answer.

Wren, Cliff's head of security, appeared by my side. She looked horrible, with a large bruise on the cheek, along with several other scrapes. Her immaculate uniform was torn with various large stains of blood. She caught me staring and then helped me to my feet. "Don't worry about it, most of it isn't mine." She grinned like this whole thing was fun for her. I was glad my claws had retracted, so I didn't have to explain their existence, but my torn clothes exposed my pregnancy.

The guard spoke with authority she apparently was used to. "I am Wren Fields, Chief of Security. These men," she pointed to various men and women, some standing while others were being loaded in ambulances, still others in police vehicles, "Broke into Mr. Clifford Matthew's estate. Using some kind of audio weapon, the assailants were able to render my male staff unable to resist."

I would never want to be on the wrong side of that woman's ire. I may have claws, but I wasn't so sure she couldn't chew nails if she desired. She obviously took a lot of pride in her team and for them to be disabled so quickly didn't sit well with her. She continued her recount of events. "They shot Mr. Matthews and his guests, then were attempting to flee with his wife. My brain screamed, *his wife*, but I have long since learned not to offer the police information. I kept my mouth closed. The guard continued to speak, "Mr. Clifford Matthew informed me his cousin Ricardis Mathews has broken into the estate, rendered his guards unable to function, and attempted to kidnap Cliff's wife. In addition, Michael Matthews, another cousin, showed up and threatened to kill their unborn children. I noticed she didn't clarify whose children were, but I remained quiet. Last, three masked assailants broke in and began shooting. He shot Mr.

Matthew's guests and rendered Ms. Rachel unconscious. One of them then dragged her out of the house. Ricky M. and Mr. King attacked the assailant and rescued Ms. Rachel. One of the assailants knocked Mr. King unconscious, but Mr. Matthews continued to fight, although he received several gunshots. The assailant finally fled to a waiting vehicle. We have visual proof of all this and will deliver the proof to the precinct within the hour. I proposed either you take her with you into custody until we can solve this matter or allow me and my guards to accompany her to the hospital."

Both of them turned to stare at me. I was soon in the car with various guards, all of them equipped with nose guards so that my pheromones didn't affect them, thanks to my advice. We rode in silence, and I wondered how did my life got here? Did that man say I was married to Clifford, a man I only met five minutes ago? What has Ricky done? Is Ricky even alive? Are any of them alive? How many children am I carrying? Are they children or puppies? I closed my eyes and longed for my life with Shane again. All the stress of the past couple of days came crashing down on me and I fell into a deep sleep. My last memory was being in the car with men I don't know. It may have been a side effect of the months I spent with Ricky M, but it was not a natural sleep.

Chapter 16
Hell and Family

Prying open my eyes, I tried to look around, but everything was dark. Could it be I was dead and in Hell? I guess I should have guessed that is where I would go. Resigned, I thought, let me find what horrors await me. After all, I deserve it. Reluctantly, I began reaching out to find the end of the bed, my fingers gripped the end of the mattress, then I swung my feet around to the end. I hoped there was a floor, or would I just keep falling into invisible flames below? With it being Hell, that would be likely, but nope, there is a floor, and it is cold. That doesn't seem right. I got a little religious education from what I knew, everything would be hot. Ok, I thought everything was fire and brimstone. Where was the smell of sulfur? All I smell is some antiseptic fragrance, maybe I haven't reached that stage yet. Putting my hands out to extend my fingers into the dark, hoping to find the end of the bed to guide me away from it. I cleared the bed, extended my hands out and touched a face. I screamed, and a male voice screamed as well. He screamed, "Lights on." A room lit up. To my surprise, I was standing by a hospital bed in a furnished room with a dresser and two comfortable looking chairs. One of which probably pulls out to a bed. I noted a window with black curtains drawn shut. Closer observations revealed just enough of a gap to see there was a moonless, dark sky. How long have I been here? Turning to look at the screamer, to my shock, it was Ralph. He was rubbing his right eye where I apparently poked him with my fingers. Realizing my Hell would not likely contain Ralph, I had to reassess my location. Meanwhile, I mumbled, "I'm sorry, Ralph. I didn't know where I was." Scrambling over to him, I moved his hand to check the level of damage I caused. His eye was red and tearing up. I spotted a small bathroom and walked into it. Finding a washcloth wetting it, I put it on the lid of the damaged orb. He said, "You know, you could have just turned on the lights yourself." I didn't answer. How could I tell him the truth? "Where are we?" That was a more sensible question, I surmised. He replied, "You certainly make an entrance, sister." I sat down on the bed. "Say what?" He said, "Well, let me back up. You have been here for three days. The doctors had to get your fluids back up, and the IVs came out a few hours ago. You are in Clifford's mansion because a judge has declared you are his legal wife since we all witnessed your wedding. He recorded your agreement to the marriage contract. Ricky M is in police custody, but he is in Critical Condition. They charged him with breaking and entry, attempted kidnapping, resisting arrest, and several other charges. I am sure his money will get him off of soon enough if he lives. The doctors ran various tests on you and the children. You are carrying triplets, just like my Marilyn, and since we are siblings, they will be cousins." "Wait!" I shouted. "This is more than I can process." He looked at me patiently, waiting for me to catch up. "How long was I with Ricky and how far along am I?" Ralph adjusted himself in his chair, and anger crossed his face. "I'm good at infiltration, but that man is down fright paranoid. I couldn't get you out." I slid off the bed and held his hand. I don't blame you. I was arrogant and foolish to walk right into his hands. Besides, I don't hate Ricky. I just thought I could overpower him. This more than likely explains why I am not susceptible to your charms, even though you waved your little tits in my face. They just do nothing for me, not like my Marilyn. The deal the two of you made still works for Clifford." Ralph stopped talking and waited for my response. I just stared at him like he had two heads. It was a couple of minutes before I could get my brain to stop whirling. "We have the same parents?" I whispered. Ralph looked annoyed. "Keep up, Sis. I will look out for you. We will discuss our parents another time. Believe me, those two are no prize. As I was saying, I will guard and care for you, sister." Tears came to my eyes.

I never had a brother or anyone looking out for me like him before. As I was just trying to digest this information, the screen on the wall slid down and the icon indicating a waiting caller appeared. I swung my head to look at my brother to see his reaction. After all, I am still a little groggy. He just shrugged, and we both waited for the caller to appear on the screen. Moments later, a woman of about 60 appeared wearing a white lab coat. She sat behind a desk. "My name is Doctor Kinney. I have been called in to consult on your case. Looking down at a screen, she read off my diagnosis. Much of what was said, Ralph had already told me. However, she added that my metabolism was significantly higher than normal. She was unsure if it had to do with my unusual pregnancy or not. Apparently, I passed out because I needed a lot more calories, she had to pump my body full of as many calories as they could. So she recommended additional supplements and told me to make sure I ingest about three to three and a half thousand calories daily. Once she wrapped up, I was exhausted. I'm not sure what to do about them. I climbed back into bed.

The drugs, or exhaustion, overcame me, closing my eyes and said that is for another day. When I woke again, Mrs. Miller was in the bed next to mine. I guess they rolled it in here when I was asleep, and she didn't look well. I sat up and really looked at the room. It was a bright strawberry color with pictures of landscapes of forests on the walls. That was the current rage today. The windows were the kind that tinted with the sun and darkened at night on their own. There was no need for curtains, but they blend well with the landscape of the walls. All of this to remind us we must protect the planet. There was no carpet but what appeared to be a hardwood floor. Considering the rest of the room, I'm sure it was some eco-friendly version of wood. I looked at my friend, and they bandaged her around the head, with only a closed eye peaking out. She looked so small, that was strange. I never thought of her as small or fragile ever before, but now she was both. I got out of bed, looking down to see myself dressed in a modest nightgown. It is not like I really care anymore if I am dressed or not. I have no modesty left, but I figure she might. I stood over her and tapped her on the shoulder as I spoke in hushed tones, "Mrs. Miller." She groaned, but no other response. "Mrs. Miller," I repeated. Still nothing. Oh, well, I'll leave her be. I turned and was heading out the door. *I'm leaving this popsicle stand*, I thought. *I can do crazy by myself.* I opened the door and heard the voice faintly, then it gained strength. "Don't leave, Rachel Lynn. I need your help." That stopped me dead in my tracks. I turned back and the elderly woman's eye was open and staring at me. I closed the door and stepped by into the room. "What would you need from me?" I walked over to her and sat on her bed. She was so small now there was plenty of room for us both. She was so weak but gave me a smile, saying, "It has been so much fun and stressful working to uncover all the things I have with the Matthews' men. You have given this old woman the adventure of a lifetime.

I have loved every bit. I need you to continue on the path. My Steven was the last of my family line. You are the closest I have ever come to having a daughter, and I want you to stay with me until I am gone." I didn't like any of this, but I learned the hard way never to interrupt my elders, so I held my tongue. She faded out like she was going to sleep. I was going to get back to my bed when her eyes opened again. She grabbed my hands and said, "As you can guess, I am dying. It wasn't the hit in the head, although that didn't help. We had a meeting a few days ago, and I was going to tell you about it. I legally adopted you. You are my heir. I am not wealthy like your husband." She said this word with disgust but continued, "However, it is a tidy passive income. I want you to work with Marilyn, Adam, John, and your brother. They are good people and have been through losses like you. This family you are married into are truly disturbing, but they do good things, too. They all have corporate schools in their territories that are downright impressive. They have rules they follow amongst themselves, but their ethics are questionable. You are on the inside now, and you have access to Thomas. This is so much bigger than you. This is the time to make a difference. Cliff ensures me he wouldn't allow Ricky or Matthew to get close to the children again. He could only get to you this time because he had just solidified the marriage by minutes before they came crashing in. I made you a video on what I know about the men as a guideline. The AI in the top drawer by your bed has all the codes we thought you would need. You can call Cliff when you are ready to meet your son." I was fighting back tears. There were so many emotions. I want to see my son. Mrs. Miller must live. I want to run and run. Rubbing my belly, I notice that it looks like it has grown larger in the last few days. "How are my babies? Did the doctors run a test?" She smiled and put her hand in mine. "They are beautiful and healthy, Honey. You fainted that day, probably all the stress of that day. I looked at her and waited until the right time to ask what I wanted to know. She beat me to the punch. "I have about six weeks to live. I will lose cognitive functions in about two. We have that time to go over the material. Then you and Marilyn can work on it. I understand Ralph wants you to approach her after she gives birth. That is probably for the best, considering her age. I would suggest you keep your pregnancy as under wraps as much as possible. Definitely take Cliff up on the guards and Honey, be sure to continue to test your limits, Ricky M put a lot of interesting things in your DNA.

Never forget you are a woman, but you are so much more. Your children will be remarkable. I will watch from heaven over the children with you." I couldn't hold back. The tears flowed because I was not a crier. In walked Ralph. He looked at me, then at Mrs. Miller. He mumbled something about "Pregnant women, and turned around and walked out." I shrugged and got in bed with her, and we held each other like that for a long time until there were no more tears. Then I finally got out and walked around in search of clothes. Ralph walked back in, took one look at me and said good. You are ready to talk. "Cliff is bringing your son in. Get dressed." He handed me a pair of jeans, panties, bra, shirt, socks, and shoes. "Go take a shower." I walked off, "Bossy much," but went off, forgetting to shut the door. He looked at my strip and said, "You know you are going to need to get used to shutting that door, succubus. I hate to stop some orderly from jerking off!" I gave him the finger as I got into the shower. It felt good to have a brother. I washed quickly, came out and was ready. Ralph led me down to the foyer. I was a little surprised at how big this house is. I mean, I knew it was the same house, just a different wing, but it was huge. There stood my boy. He was beautiful. I could see my eyes and chin in him, and I believe they used Shane's sperm. I could see Shane's color and hair. We did not conceive this child, but I love him. The woman holding his hand was a woman in her mid-60s with gray hair tied neatly in a bun. She was tall and round, with a very pleasant face. She introduced herself as Audrey, the nanny. I held my hand out and said, "My name is Jack. Nice to meet you." She looked at me curiously, like everyone else does, but I ignored it. Bending down to speak, I greeted my son, "Hello, and what name do you go by?" He looked at me fearlessly and said, "I am Tom for Thomas, are you my Mommy?" Smiling so much, it was a chance my face could split. "I am, and I came a long way to find you. I will never leave you now that I have found you. May I touch you by giving you a kiss?" He looked at me like I had grown an extra head. "Of course, that is what Mommies are supposed to do." "Well, I never knew my Mommy, so you may have to help me. Then I just found my brother Ralph yesterday. Our mommy left him too, you might have to teach him to be an uncle." He smiled and whispered conspiratorial, "That's ok. Daddy is not really my daddy, he is my brother. I am teaching him how to act like a daddy, too." I smiled, "Well, I am sure you are a brilliant teacher."

We were mostly inseparable after that. I still need Audrey because of my advanced pregnancy and the three children coming. She was wonderful. Ralph and I spoke daily. Mrs. Miller did decline after two weeks and went into a coma on the third. She passed away in the fourth week. That was hard, but having my son made life bearable. I saw very little of Clifford, that was a relief. He took me to the tours of the schools. I guess for publicity, Thomas and I didn't interact with anyone. We barely spoke. I got to see Marilyn but followed the rules and didn't speak to her while she was pregnant. I wore clothing that made it difficult to see I was pregnant. It wasn't hard to fool them because the people here didn't know me. The more I learned about Cliff and his cousins, the more I disliked this bunch of privileged, spoiled men. They were playing with other's lives like pieces on a chessboard. They are utterly ruthless, with no regard for the well-being of others. Ricky M believes he loves me, and in his way, he does. I wouldn't recognize it until Shane taught me true love. However, Ricky and Matthew have both recovered, then the police released them. They are both quiet or at least Cliff hasn't told me anything. So, I have been leading a low-stress life. I will give my children and my nieces and nephews all the love I never had. Tonight, Marilyn went into labor, and the men have planned for me to sneak in and remain all night with Marilyn. I was there just after they delivered the babies. I was so eager to just wrap my arms around her. The timing was still not right. I held my nieces and nephews while I dressed in a nurse's scrubs as a disguise. I laid the children in her arms and whispered to her, we have to talk. Tonight, I will be back. She nodded, and I left.

Later that night, Ralph escorted me into the room. The three cribs were all lined up together with oxygen pumps attached. Marilyn woke when we entered. There was a guard in the room that permitted us inside. She smiled at me and I smiled back. Ralph said,

"Marilyn, I would like to introduce you to my sister, Rachel. She goes by Jack." I saw the shock on her face.

Ralph explained, "I only found out about my sister a few weeks ago, but she is in a lot of trouble. I asked her not to introduce herself until you delivered. She needs our help. She also very much wants to get to know her nephews and nieces and for you to know her child and soon-to-be children. You have met Thomas. He is my nephew as well." I again saw the surprise, but she waited patiently. "She is also carrying three more children. They are Cliff's cousin Ricky M's biological children. Cliff married her to keep Ricky M from imprisoning and raping her again and his brother Michael from stealing her children. Marilyn gasp.

Ralph said, "A long story. Suffice it to say Cliff's cousins will come after her again. She is due in a few months. I looked at this woman that appears to be about the same age as Ralph, in her early sixty's. She is one of the several women that over the typical childbearing age, choosing to give birth again. I don't know if I would be that brave or selfless, but she has my respect. Ralph, apparently, sees her as some kind of miracle worker as he dumped my problems in her lap. He was still explaining my situation to her. "Ricky's lawyers have claimed his parental rights to ensure he can be there for the birth of his children. They also claim the marriage to Clifford is a sham. He has a legal contract under North Carolina law, by her confirmation of his relationship as her mate." I said, "I know this is a lot to dump on you, and I am sorry.

He changed my DNA to make me Trans-species. I am his mate and he can prove it in court. I can't deny it. What can we do? Marilyn said, "Wow, this is a lot. We will have a lot to work on. Of course, we will. It is nice to meet you, dear. When can we meet again? "When you are up to it, Cliff's mansion or around him is the safest place for me to be. I dislike that man beyond belief, but he has never hurt me, so I stay.

As a matter of fact, I think he avoids me, which suits me fine."
Marilyn said, "Well, then, I am sure there is a lot more for you to tell
me because that man is too slimy to hide from a beautiful woman."
Ralph interrupted, "I will fill you in on our little succubus here." I
turned to him. "Will you stop calling me that?"

He said, "Um, does it bother you?" I said, "Yeah." Laughing,
"Well, absolutely, 'Not' in that case," Marilyn laughed. "Welcome to
having brothers." I joined in the laughter. Her hands went to her
belly and she said, laughing hurts right now. I looked at her still
smiling face and knew right then I would come to love her. I put my
hand softly on hers and told her thank you and good night. Ralph
ushered me out of the room.

Chapter 17
Unexpected Future

Over the next few months, I spent a great deal of time with Marilyn and her children. I've never felt part of a family before, and I love it. The only thing I don't like is the fact I need guards and arrangements have to be made everywhere I go. However, Marilyn understands and is under guard as well. My son Thomas is a pure joy. He and his nanny, Audrey, have been so special to me. She is teaching me how to raise children. I absolutely would be lost without her. We three are inseparable. Cliff is always busy. I only see him at a meal, maybe two or three times a week, and our periodic visits to his corporate schools. He speaks to Thomas and Audrey but barely looks at me. The recordings left by Mrs. Miller and stories told me by Adam, John, Ralph, and Marilyn make me not like the man, anyway. However, we need each other. I can stop him from being manipulated by Ricky, but the war between Ricky and Matthew hinges on Cliff keeping me. I am married to a man I hate, but this is the safest place to be. Not to mention, I still do not know who the leather-faced intruders were and why they were trying to abduct me. Michael and Ricky each made a miraculous recovery. Each had several gunshot wounds and were admitted to private hospitals, where I am told they each made recoveries. Cliff told me the medical personnel were stunned at their recovery and had to be paid to keep it quiet. Michael needed a little more time in the hospital, but Ricky was released. Their miracle would not have been possible if it weren't for this so-called serum in their bloodstream. Cliff also said he has been negotiating with his brothers to make it clear that no harm will come to his wife, and she has the freedom to leave if she chooses.

Months later:

217

I am huge, I can't see my feet, I have to pee every fifteen minutes, I'm constantly eating, and I am tired a lot. My aching body needs me to take several naps a day and be in bed alone for the night, around eight every night. I am blessed that Audrey is here to care for Thomas because I can't. One night, a hand covered my mouth and I woke. I can't jump and fight like before, but my claws will work. Moments before my claws emerged from my skin, the familiar scent hit me first. My body responded, and my sleepy mind registered, "Mate." Out of the darkness came a familiar voice. "It's me. Please put your claws away. I'm not here to take you anywhere, and I could never hurt you." The hand moved away. "I will leave if you want me too, but I ask for you to please hear me out?" I sat up. "No, don't sit up, relax and lay back. You are so beautiful. I will lie beside you." He lay down and, wrapped his arm around my enormous belly, and kissed my shoulders. Ricky breathed into my back. "Cliff and I have been talking by text. He doesn't trust me visually, but he permitted me to visit with you. You and your first husband were the topics of our discussions. He helped me see my approach with you and the other women's mates was wrong. I truly didn't understand before, but now I do now. I am sorry for my tunnel vision. I caused the death of Shane and many others.

Although I didn't give the orders for the men to be held and milked for their genetic material, it was under my watch. I've been cleaning the house and will continue for some time to do so. My tunnel vision has always been a handicap for me. Not giving you a choice or freedom because of my own insecurities was wrong. When you tried to warn me about the men who worked for me, I didn't listen. I was so jealous. I just couldn't. My company hired subcontractors to work for me, and I don't even know their real names. Nor did I care, barely recognizing them as humans. To try to mend my wrongs, I tracked down the company I used, but they said they didn't send anyone out. They, in fact, say I haven't used their agency for over two years. Someone has been using their name, sending out people. With the masks, I couldn't tell one from the other. Whoever is running the operation has their own agenda. Sandy Beaudreux and her husband have gone missing as well. They were in charge of my IVF clinic in North Carolina. It was the main depository for the genetic material collected from my smaller sites. They seemed to be running some kind of scheme to sell genetic material. I'm sorry, I wasn't focused on what was happening under my nose, and people like you were hurt." He rubbed my belly and was kissing my arm up to my neck. I sighed. "You feel good. I miss you." Turning over in his arms, I said. "I was so scared that I killed you. I didn't mean to." He kissed my lips. "I know, but I made all the mistakes. I should have known you can't be caged that long. Now, because of me, you have to be guarded. Another form of cage. I should have let you go and hoped you came back to me." He moved my gown up as his hand continued to slide up my thighs. I kissed him back, finding I missed him, and asked, "What about Michael? Does he still want to take our children?" Ricky moaned, "Yes, Cliff has been trying to talk him down. My other two brothers are also negotiating this problem. Do you feel safe here? Do you want to stay?" He kissed me again as he ran his fingers along the seam of my panties. My body and mind responded to my mate. I could barely think to answer, "I am safe here, and Thomas is here. Cliff is his guardian and he said it is too dangerous for both of us to leave. He refuses to allow our son to leave, but he says he can't hold me. I won't ever leave my son."

Ricky M's eyes show love and remorse, saying, "The understanding look was new on him. He was truly trying to be a better person for me. Staring at my lips, I could read the desires on his face that were saying, I want you so badly. Licking his own lips, he not only drew my eyes but my desires, "I love children and will raise Thomas and our triplets with you, here, if Cliff permits.

If you tell me you want to go, I will," he said. I bit my lip. His eyes followed, and then his body jerked like it was taking everything inside of him to resist assaulting me. Maybe he really has learned his lesson, and I am so hormonal. My cravings for his touch were just as hard to hold back. I pushed him back from me. The disappointed look he gave was so sincere. With great difficulty, I rolled until I could get myself off the bed. Soon, I was standing in front of him. He was wearing similar clothing as he was the last day I saw him. His crooked arm was under his head, and he looked as though he was not looking forward to leaving. Lifting my gown over the head, my panties dropped to the floor, his eyes widened. I looked at my mate and his expression had changed to pure joy. He opened his arms to welcome me, and for the first time, we made love as partners. Call me crazy, but I think I love this man. He is not Shane. By comparison, he is damaged, however we fit. We slept in each other's arms. I woke on his chest in the morning, but this time, the sun was shining through an enormous window and I could leave out. I will never forget Shane. At the end of his life, he taught what love looks like. My relationship with Ricky M is not ideal and few would understand it, but I need him. He and I agree that I will live with and stay married to Cliff for both the safety of myself and Thomas.

Number 2

I wake up cold and my shoulders are sore. The two-legged furless have taken me away from my pack and Mommy. I haven't been alone since my eyes opened, and now I am cold as well. I can't get out and run, either. Crying is all I can do, I'm so lonely and scared. The loud sounds are scary, but nothing is as bad as the movement. The rocking is making my ... Too late, there goes my breakfast and I can't even move from it. Finally, we stop. The two-legged furless picks me up and strokes my back. I looked into his eyes, and I knew, "Alpha." He put me on sweet-smelling grass. The breeze brought the smells all around. The movement had me jerking my head to the woods and I took off to chase it. The moist ground, the wind in my fur and my tongue lolling out were euphoric. Alpha ran with me as we corned the creature. It skittered up a tree half a second before my jaws could snap shut. Alpha commanded me to sit, and I did so and received the tasty snack. Given half a chance, I would eat everything at once, but he doesn't give me the opportunity. It was one of those days when the sun was high in the sky and the smells were full, it was glorious. A new sound hit me first, then smells of a new two-legged. Pack. Sniffing all the two-legged, I come to a cub. He smelled like pack, he picked me up, I knew I would protect him all my life.

The End

Epilogue 1

Audrey and I were sitting on a bench outside the house, overlooking the expanse of greenery in the back of the mansion. It was that time of year when the trees had turned colors just before the leaves fell. There was so much natural beauty, and Thomas just loved to run. To see the joy on his face makes all the aches and pains from my advanced pregnancy seem so remote. His joy continues to remind me of what I missed out on in my childhood. I swear to myself right now I will never willingly abandon any of my children. Rubbing my belly, using my inner voice, I made that promise. I was content. Ricky M. has been back at his home for about two weeks now but speaks to me several times a day. He even calls Thomas on his AI and gives him words of encouragement. The two of them are designing a replica of the Mars colony. Thomas is learning history and science, and I don't know which one of them enjoys it more. Right now, Thomas is playing a holographic game with his AI based on the colony, a reworking of the game hide and seek. "ARF, ark," broke into my musing. I turned to stare at Audrey to see if she heard it, too, and she was looking at me, questioning the same. "ARF," there it was again. Moments later, a little fur ball came sniffing at my feet. It was snow-white with a large red bow tied to its neck and so furry that it was hardly recognizable as a dog. I jumped to move my feet, but Audrey reached down to pick it up. With the size of my belly, I couldn't reach down there if I tried, and I could jump up just in my seat. "All, where did you come from, precious?" Audrey said as she stroked its fur. Moments later, Thomas was at her side, staring at the puppy with awe. Thomas's eyes looked behind Audrey and me and exclaimed, "You did it. Is he mine?" The grin splitting his face was contagious. I found myself and Audrey smiling before we understood what we were agreeing to. Now it clicked, "Wait, what?" I turned around and both Cliff and Ricky M were standing behind us, staring at Thomas. Trying to get up was slow, and then Ricky was in front of me, pulling me into his arms and stealing a kiss. He laughingly said, "Every boy should have a dog." Looking at him, then to our boy, it was too late to take it away now. In hushed tones, I said, "I wish the two of you had said something to me first. I have never had pets and have no idea how to take care of him." Cliff spoke up now, "We will teach you as well as train him, although you will need to learn German commands." Since Cliff never jokes, all I can do is accept his words at face value. "Well, why not?" I responded. This is already an unconventional family as it is. We all went into the house, Ricky had his arm around my expanded waist, Cliff was carrying Thomas had the puppy in his arms. Then Audrey followed up the rear. The puppy squirmed in the thin arms of Thomas, then began licking his face. Thomas giggled as he turned his face to dodge the little tongue of the pup. He asked, "Uncle Ricky, what's his name? Ricky was smiling as well, seeing my boy with the dog seemed to delight him. I call him Aussie. However, you can name him whatever you choose. We will be working with training him. He has already learned some command words in both German and English. Thomas's little face frowned up as he thought about this. With the seriousness of a child, he said, "I like the name Aussie, thank you, Uncle." Ricky turned to look at my smiling face and said in a low voice, Aussie has been altered to be stronger and more intelligent than an average dog. Don't forget, we need him as a companion and guard for all of our children. I turned to kiss him. I liked how he referred to Thomas as one of our children. We all went back into the house happily, and I headed straight for the bathroom to pee again.

Epilogue 2

Ahhhhhh, No, I can't believe it! I was fifteen when I went into the sleep chamber, and now I am biologically twenty and on the Mars colony. Why didn't I read the side effects of the long sleep? Just being chosen was such an honor, then all the tests and training. Maybe I should cut myself some slack, but this is not at all what I pictured that I would look like when I woke up. My face was devoid of hair. I mean, there were no eyebrows or nose hairs, let alone on the top of my head. My skin was saggy as though I aged sixty years, not five. I stared in disbelief. How many shocks can I take? I woke from a five-year sleep, and I started vomiting in front of this really cute nurse or whatever her title is. Then, she gave me a tablet and asked me to verify my information. Scanning through it, I confirmed I was Randall Cobble, here on Mars, to train being a doctor. Then, bizarrely, it listed Ralph and Beulah King as my parents. Not the Cobbles that brought me home from the hospital to raise me. Lastly, she thrusts a mirror in my face and I see my appearance. After all those shocks, now my dick is hard. What's next?

About The Author

I grew up in a few different states and in the United Kingdom. My father was in the military and we traveled a bit. My family settled in Southern Maryland where I raised a family and still reside. Books have always been the constant in my life allowing me to enjoy different lives and worlds alike. I enjoyed writing this book series as it allowed my active imagination to soar.

Don't miss out!

Visit the website below and you can sign up to receive emails whenever LaneyC publishes a new book. There's no charge and no obligation.

https://books2read.com/r/B-A-BYGX-KVVKC

BOOKS 2 READ

Connecting independent readers to independent writers.

Milton Keynes UK
Ingram Content Group UK Ltd.
UKHW040637131123
432470UK00001B/112